WITH A TRUSTING HEART

DAWN KINZER

Morningview Publishing

Scripture quotations are from the King James Version of the Bible.

This story was inspired by events that took place during the Alaska-Yukon-Pacific Exposition in 1909—the setting, people, and history. However, this is still a work of fiction and the product of the author's imagination.

Cover design by Lynnette Bonner of Indie Cover Design – https://www.indiecoverdesign.com

Images©
https://www.shutterstock.com/Photo ID 451849768/model
Photo of Brown Hall, Public Domain

With a Trusting Heart/Dawn Kinzer
ISBN: 978-1-7367770-3-9

For all the orphans in the world

and those who love and protect them.

Trust in the Lord with all thine heart;
and lean not unto thine own understanding.
In all thy ways acknowledge him,
and he shall direct thy paths.

~ Proverbs 3:5–6

One

Taking a firm stance, she raised her hands and aimed at the mess created that morning. If only the clutter would disappear with the move of her trigger finger.

Lizzie Clark dropped the imaginary pistols into the invisible holster hung around her hips and chuckled to herself. Perhaps she'd gotten too caught up in the excitement of several boys anticipating the Wild West Show later that day at the Alaska-Yukon-Pacific Exposition.

She assessed the stacked breakfast dishes on the kitchen counter, ready to be washed and dried. If she worked fast and hard enough, she might have five minutes to enjoy a cup of tea before tackling the next job on her list.

Helen Caswell, the head cook, nodded toward the pile of dirty plates, bowls, pots, and pans. "Taking on that job alone today was a kind thing to do."

"It didn't feel right to ask Emma to stay behind." Lizzie picked up a dishrag and leaned against the sink. "The girl is only seventeen, and someone who works as hard as she does deserves a little fun. Besides, we won't have as many to feed for lunch with the majority of Brown Hall's residents attending the fair."

Lizzie had already grown fond of the quiet young woman with blond hair, striking amber eyes, and a nose too large for her face. Emma Johnson worked in the kitchen as part of her training to leave the orphanage, and she hoped to find employment at a restaurant or with a wealthy family.

A meek soul, she rarely talked, but Lizzie and Helen were trying to instill confidence in her. Emma's mother had died, and her father had lost his job. He'd promised to come for her once he got back on his feet, but in the five years Emma had lived at the orphanage, he'd never returned even once to check on her. No wonder she thought little of herself.

During Children's Day at the expo, the twenty-five-cent admission for youth was waived, so today was a perfect opportunity for the orphans from Brown Hall to visit. This world's fair, held on the University of Washington's grounds, had opened up new experiences to the people of Seattle and those traveling great distances to attend.

Having only moved from Portland and begun her new job three weeks ago, Lizzie hadn't ventured to the fair yet. Of course she was anxious to see the sights, but the exposition would remain open for another two months, so there was plenty of time to enjoy the attractions.

Volunteers from a nearby church would help chaperone the seventy-four children on the walk to the fair and stay with them throughout the day. The entrance to the expo took only five minutes via trolley, but it was important to save the five-cent fare. Donations had given the youngsters, ages five through sixteen, enough money to purchase lemonade and a frankfurter. Lizzie and Helen would make lunch for the fifteen children aged four and under who remained behind, but the nursery matron would make sure the five babies were provided nourishment. They'd have supper ready for all when the fairgoers returned.

As a teacher at Brown Hall, her brother fed minds, but Lizzie was currently helping to nourish the bodies of the orphans and the adults who cared for them, and that brought her great satisfaction.

"My goodness, the children are in for an adventure." Helen kneaded the third batch of bread dough with a steady rhythm, the heels of her hands pushing the dough down and then outward. "The excitement generated the last twenty-four hours could have supplied enough energy to clean the entire building from top to bottom if we'd had a hankering to put the youngsters to work. I don't think Rachel slept but a few minutes all night."

Lizzie smiled at the mention of the mischievous seven-year-old with long dark braids and a missing front tooth. "Their enthusiasm is understandable. My brother has been sharing some interesting facts about the expo during their classes—all educational, of course." Lizzie winked. "At breakfast, the boys were challenging each other to ride the Ferris wheel."

"One of the older boys was taunting Rachel about some ride called the Haunted Swing." Helen shook her head. "Oh, my . . . what are we going to be dealing with tonight? Nightmares?"

"I wouldn't worry," Lizzie said, brushing back loose curls of hair from where they'd fallen over her eyes. "The chaperones will keep a close watch on each child, and my brother has an itinerary that he expects everyone to follow. For Timothy to get approval for this outing, he had to assure the state superintendent for Washington Children's Home Society that he'd use the opportunity as part of his teaching curriculum."

Helen folded the dough in half, then pressed down on the mixture again. "Ah, leave it to Mr. L. J. Covington to require that any activity be associated with learning."

"They'll have a great time playing on the Pay Streak, and their other encounters will be exciting *and* enlightening. Exposure to other countries like Japan, Turkey, Greece, Germany, Great Britain, France, Sweden, China . . . the superintendent won't have anything to complain about."

The Pay Streak was the exposition's midway area. For a price, it offered a dizzying array of carnival rides, quasi-educational exhibits, souvenirs, and refreshments. Lizzie was prepared for the attendees to be either worn out by the time they returned, or so exhilarated, they'd chatter for hours about everything they'd seen and done.

The outside screen door to the kitchen slammed, drawing the women's attention.

Helen grabbed a towel and wiped the excess flour from her hands. "Emma, aren't you supposed to be on your way to the fair with the children?"

"I'll catch up to them." The girl's mesmerizing eyes were filled with questions. "I—I didn't know what to do. We'd barely left when a young woman I've never seen before approached me." Emma held up a wicker basket covered with a blue blanket. "She handed me this and a note and said to give them to you, Lizzie."

"Me? Why?" And why wouldn't a gift be brought directly to her?

"The only explanation she gave was that she'd been asked by her neighbor Nellie to make the delivery. And when I peeked inside . . . I called for her to come back. *I did.*" Emma's eyes pooled. "But she was gone so fast."

"You did nothing wrong." Helen put an arm around the girl's shoulders. "Now, let's take a look."

Lizzie removed the basket from Emma's arms and lifted the thin, clean white blanket to see a sleeping newborn.

Two

"Oh, my . . ." Lizzie's heart melted at seeing the innocent baby. She peeked beneath the child's clothing. "A boy. He must belong to Nellie Wick. But why bring him here—to me?"

Helen gently caressed the sleeping infant's cheek. "The woman you befriended at the train station—the lady who sells flowers to travelers?"

"Yes. She expected to deliver within the next several weeks, and there's no other explanation." A horrible truth struck Lizzie like a stone fired from one of the orphans' slingshots. "Nellie would never have abandoned her child unless she believed she had no other choice. Unless she didn't mean to give him up. Perhaps she only needs help for a short time."

"Talk to Nellie. Find out her true intention," Helen said.

Lizzie groaned. "I never asked about her accommodations. I didn't want to be nosy, but that concern seems so foolish now." Her heart pounded. "I'll find the person who brought the child and insist she take me to Nellie." Lizzie set the basket on the kitchen table. Never mind that the tabletop was covered in flour. They'd tidy up later.

"Go! The baby is fine with me." Helen opened the screen door that led to the side yard. "Emma, you too. There's still time to catch up with the group if you hurry."

"Maybe I should stay and help you look for her." Emma

chewed her lower lip. "I'm so sorry. If I'd known, I would have told the stranger I couldn't take the basket—that she needed to speak to you."

"None of this is your fault." Lizzie gave the girl a reassuring hug. "You did a great deed in bringing the baby to me. I'm grateful for your help. But I insist you go to the fair and then come home and tell me *everything*." Lizzie led the way outside, and they raced down the steps. "Now, what did the woman look like?"

"A little older than me. Blond hair. She wore a gray skirt and jacket."

"Which direction did she go?"

Emma pointed to the left.

Though she ran for two blocks, Lizzie couldn't find the person Emma described. She'd disappeared, and Lizzie had no idea of where to search for her. With a heavy heart, she trudged back to Brown Hall.

Named after founders Reverend Harrison D. Brown and his wife Libbie Beach Brown, the enormous three-story brick building with six large white pillars spread across the wide front porch had been built a year ago after the original home at Green Lake was destroyed by fire. The new building housed nearly a hundred children and the adults who cared for them. Although the reverend and his wife continued to oversee the orphanage, he also took on ministerial responsibilities at a local Methodist church, and she continued to speak in churches on behalf of children.

Lizzie had spoken to Nellie about the reverend and his wife and how much she admired them. Although, tragically, little ones were often thought of as being expendable, the couple shared a different view. They believed all children should be loved and protected. Reverend and Mrs. Brown sincerely cared about the living conditions in existing orphanages, and they'd begun implementing their new idea of placing orphans for adoption in family foster homes rather than in institutions.

Was that why the new mother had left her son with Lizzie? She trusted that her baby would be safe at Brown Hall? Was she also so desperate that she felt there was no alternative for her? "Oh, Nellie . . ."

Knowing the baby was coming soon, Lizzie had planned to check on her friend tomorrow at the train station where she worked. Perhaps Nellie only needed temporary care for the infant. If so, why didn't she merely ask for help?

Lizzie, feeling defeated at not finding the woman who had delivered the little boy to the orphanage, discovered Helen still in the kitchen watching over the sleeping child. He looked content as he slumbered peacefully, his lashes resting on his pink cheeks. Dark hair, like his mother's, covered his tiny head. How could anyone abandon such a sweet gift?

Helen poured two cups of coffee, handed one to Lizzie, then sat in a wooden chair next to the table. "You didn't find the neighbor?"

"No." Lizzie sipped the hot liquid. "I ran for blocks, but there wasn't a sign of her anywhere. The baby wasn't supposed to come for several more weeks. I'm hoping Nellie only left him with us because she needed more time to prepare."

Helen raised her eyebrows.

"You don't think that's what happened, do you?" Lizzie searched the woman's eyes for an answer.

"A letter was left behind." Helen reached for the envelope sitting next to the basket and handed it to Lizzie. "I haven't opened it, but I'm assuming it will answer some of your questions."

She slit open the envelope, removed the thin piece of paper, and read its contents silently.

Dear Lizzie,

Forgive me, but there is much I cannot explain. I can only tell you that I have been grateful for your friendship, even in the few weeks we have known each other. It has been a gift.

Now I must ask something of you that goes beyond friendship, as I have nowhere else to turn. I am alone and unable to provide for my son in the way he deserves.

Please take care of Ernest and keep him safe. I am trusting you with the love of my life. My heart is breaking, and only by knowing that you will be watching over his best interests can I bear to part with this precious little boy.

Do all that you can to assure Ernest that I love him completely and that I will think of him every day.

Nellie

☙

Jack Butler, holding a crate of freshly picked green beans, stood on the steps leading to Brown Hall's kitchen. The heavier door had been left open, probably due to the warm August weather. He prepared to announce his presence but hearing a baby had been left at the orphanage, he hesitated.

It felt wrong to eavesdrop. He was there to deliver produce from his family's farm, and the conversation taking place inside wasn't any of his business. Jack set the crate down and knocked on the screen door.

Helen Caswell, the orphanage's head cook, swung open the door. "Come in, Jack! Nice to see you again. It's been a while."

"Good morning, Helen." He carried the beans inside and placed the large crate on a low counter near the door. "You're right. It's been at least a month since I've made any deliveries. Dad always enjoys visiting with customers, but he thought it would be good for me to take a break from the fields today."

"Well, please say hello to him." She offered a warm smile that hinted a fondness for his father then ran her fingers through the beans. "These look lovely. What else do you have for me?"

"Another box of beans, and we picked enough corn this morning for at least one meal. We'll have more next week." Jack sensed the other woman in the kitchen watching him. Since she was unfamiliar, he merely turned and gave a brief, "Good morning!" Then he headed outside to retrieve the rest of his delivery.

Jack returned, hauling a heavy crate filled with cobs of golden sweet corn. Helen had propped the door open, which made this entry easier. The ladies mentioned a woman named Nellie Wick, including some of her physical characteristics, and Jack dropped the box next to the green beans with a loud plunk. It couldn't be her—but *another* woman with that name who also had a limp and a scar? *Not likely.*

A baby in the room released a high-pitched wail.

Now he'd gone and done it! Jack turned around and approached the table where an infant's cry came from a large basket. "I'm sorry. I didn't realize—I didn't mean to make so much noise."

Helen's kitchen companion smiled, and her face lit up like the sky at dawn—beautiful and welcoming—disarming Jack for a moment. "Don't worry. You did nothing wrong. He's probably hungry or needing a change." She discreetly checked his diaper. "All dry."

"I'll warm a bottle for him," Helen said.

The other woman picked up the baby, then returned to her chair and cradled him in her arms, quieting the boy.

"Jack, Miss Clark recently joined us as a cook." Helen put her hand on the younger woman's shoulder briefly, but long enough to display affection toward her. Helen's approval revealed plenty about the new employee's character.

"I prefer informality," the pretty addition to Brown Hall said. "Please call me Lizzie."

Jack nodded. The name suited her—bright and shiny like a new penny.

Helen stepped closer. "Lizzie, you've met Jack's father, LeRoy Butler. Although they both like to keep it a secret, I think you should know that not only do they give us a discount, but they also often donate large quantities of food to the orphanage."

"How generous of you! Your father has delivered vegetables from your farm several times since I moved into Brown Hall, and he's been very kind to me."

"We're happy to help." Jack preferred to keep any good

deeds anonymous, but in this case, anyone working in the kitchen might need to understand the arrangement.

With sunlight streaming in through a nearby window, Lizzie's red hair looked like gleaming copper, and her green eyes rivaled emeralds. Jack tried not to stare at the captivating scene.

He gestured toward the child. "Your son?" Nothing should be assumed, but weren't the orphan babies kept in a nursery instead of the kitchen? And the infant had quieted down as soon as she'd placed him in her arms.

"No. His mother left him in my care, although it's still a bit confusing as to why," Lizzie said in a thoughtful whisper.

"From what you've told me, Nellie must have had good reasons," Helen said.

The boy was Nellie's? Shock hit Jack like a lightning bolt splitting a tree in half. Even though he'd heard her name mentioned earlier, the reality that *she* was the abandoned baby's mother felt absurd. What kind of desperation had driven his childhood friend to desert her son? Jack needed air. "I have more vegetables to bring in before I go."

He slipped outside and made his way to the wagon, barely conscious of what he was doing. As he placed another load on the kitchen counter, he heard the women talking.

"Since Nellie wasn't expecting to deliver her baby this soon, I'm hoping she merely felt overwhelmed and that once she has a little time to think, she'll want him back."

Jack turned and leaned against the counter. He wouldn't interrupt their conversation.

"She could return tomorrow," Helen said, sounding unconvinced.

"Or she may be too ashamed to come." Lizzie's brow

furrowed. "I have responsibilities here for the rest of the day, so I can't leave. But tomorrow is Sunday, and I'm free from working in the kitchen. After breakfast, I'll place Ernest in the nursery and then look for Nellie at the train station where she sets up shop. Hopefully, a night's rest will have given her enough time to miss him and change her mind."

"And the morning church service?" Helen asked.

"I think the good Lord will understand my missing for such an important mission."

"I agree. Our relationship with him isn't based on how many hours we spend in a pew." Helen sat in a wooden chair and placed folded hands on the table. "The baby will be safe and well-cared for by our staff, but what if his mother doesn't show up at her usual spot? What if she's not well?"

"I hadn't considered that possibility—that Nellie might have had trouble giving birth." Lizzie sighed. "Well, other vendors set up their wares at the train station. Surely someone will remember a woman with a scar and limp." She tilted her head and gazed at the child in her arms. "I have to at least try to find her."

The two cooks had probably forgotten he was in the room as they openly discussed their plans. Jack decided right then. He would arrive the next day in time to assist Lizzie in the search. Maybe there was a way he could help Nellie keep her child, if that's what she wanted.

But there was no reason to say anything to Lizzie about wanting to get involved—not until he had time to think and decide how much he wanted to disclose.

He owed Nellie for saving him years ago, and he'd do anything necessary now to prove his loyalty.

Three

L izzie set the empty bottle on the table and positioned Ernest over her shoulder. She gently patted his back until a quiet burp released.

Helen placed a steaming cup of chamomile tea in front of Lizzie. "Still want to keep him with you tonight? You won't get much sleep, if any."

"We can make room for sweet Ernest in the nursery." Nineteen-year-old Julia Meadows had helped the matron take care of the toddlers and babies for almost two years, and the gentle, kind soul nurtured the little ones.

Lizzie's brother, sitting at the table next to Julia, reached for her hand. Timothy winked at the young woman with a smattering of freckles, light brown hair, and turquoise eyes. "Since my sister has arrived, you've seen how stubborn she can be when she sets her mind to something. Hence, her insistence on roaming the city without a chaperone."

"Only when I'm confident of how to reach my destination, dear brother." Lizzie attempted her most charming smile.

Only a year apart in age, she and Timothy had always been best friends and much closer to each other than to their brother, Joseph, three years younger than Lizzie.

"Julia and the matron are already busy enough with five babies to tend to, and I don't want to add more responsibility." Lizzie cradled the back of Ernest's head in her hands, then brought him from her shoulder into a supine position in her arms. She swayed back and forth slowly, and his eyes closed as he drifted into a peaceful sleep.

"My bedroom is out of the way, and if Ernest wakes up during the night, he won't disturb the other children. But, Julia, I will need to leave the baby in the nursery tomorrow while I search for his mother. I can't imagine Nellie wanting to give him up. I've known her for less than a month, but she's honest and kind, and I can tell from her letter that she loves her little boy. It tore at her heart to leave him here. So if there's anything I can do to help her . . ."

"Of course." Julia smiled warmly. "I'll make sure he's tended to while you're gone. You won't have to worry about him."

"Thank you." Lizzie rearranged the blanket around the child. "I may seem a bit sensitive to the matter but . . ."

"Nellie protected you, and now you want to return the favor." Helen poured a spot of hot water in Lizzie's tea.

"Ernest is lucky to have you as his champion. If only other children were so fortunate," Julia said thoughtfully. "Whatever the outcome—whether you find his mother or not—I have faith that God is watching over him. Our heavenly Father wants the best for all children."

Julia was an angel. No wonder Timothy was falling in love with her—not that he'd confessed it to Lizzie. He didn't need to—she only had to observe how he looked at the young woman who had survived a difficult past.

A sunbeam could almost shine right through Julia as she was a delicate wisp of a thing. At eight years old, she had been left at an orphanage known for strict discipline. Too old for couples who wanted to adopt babies and too puny for those who wanted a laborer more than a child, Julia lived at the orphanage until seventeen and then was forced to leave. She had nowhere to go, so she inquired about work with the Children's Home Society and was hired by Reverend Brown. The opportunity had saved Julia from a life of uncertainty and homelessness on the streets.

Lizzie didn't want to think about what might happen to the baby in her arms if he grew up without a family. But with childlike faith, Julia believed God cared deeply about each soul.

Did that concern include her? She envied her brother's strong conviction that God had a plan for his life. Timothy had encouraged Lizzie to trust that their heavenly Father wanted the best for her, but one dream after another had been dashed. Perhaps she had yet to prove herself worthy.

Enough thinking about all the difficult decisions ahead. Lizzie wanted to focus on anything else, if even for a short time, and lighten the serious tone that had filled the room. "Timothy—Julia—tell me about your day at the expo. I want to hear every detail!"

❧

Lizzie studied the sleeping child nestled in his makeshift cradle next to her bed. If necessary, they'd create different accommodations later. But for now, the tiny infant fit comfortably in the wicker basket. Lizzie preferred to stretch out in bed and not be confined, but Julia had assured her that swaddling Ernest and keeping him in a small space, much like his mother's womb, would be comforting and help him feel safe.

In the soft glow emanating from a table lamp, the tiny

infant was a vision of innocence and perfection. He'd fussed for only a short time before falling asleep to Lizzie's lullabies. Fortunately, she'd thought to turn down the chimes on the mantel clock she'd brought with her—a sentimental piece inherited from her grandmother.

She discarded the temptation to pick up the child and hold him close. The chance of waking him was too great, and they both needed rest. *Careful, Lizzie.* How could she feel so attached in such a short time?

Dangerous—this feeling of wanting to mother Ernest. Lizzie hadn't come to the orphanage with any intention of finding a child to raise. She was still seeking direction for her own life. How could she possibly take on the responsibility of someone else's?

It was only after Timothy's encouragement that Lizzie decided to apply for the position of cook at Brown Hall. Not long after, she recognized how the opportunity could be fulfilling and a way for her to move on from pain and disappointments.

The move here was the first step to building a life of her own. Timothy was convinced that all she'd experienced had led her to Seattle and that God still had good things in store, despite the heartache she'd endured. Lizzie wanted to claim that belief for herself with unrelenting faith but failed most days.

Perhaps if she hadn't been let down numerous times . . . and perhaps, if Alex had lived, Lizzie wouldn't feel so hurt and abandoned. If it weren't for Timothy, she'd never have survived her loss.

Handsome, intelligent, kind—her best friend from the time they were six years old, Alex had filled Lizzie's world.

Was God so jealous of her devotion to someone else that he refused to let them live out their lives together?

No, Lizzie knew better. God's love didn't work that way, but that knowledge still didn't hinder the fire that sometimes rekindled in her belly. Pastor Martinson had assured Lizzie that God could handle her anger, so why was there never a response to her outbursts? Why had he remained silent?

Alex proposed when they were both nineteen. Not long after, he was diagnosed with tuberculosis. Lizzie had wanted to marry, regardless, believing he would get better. But he'd refused, knowing he might die and leave her a widow. Lizzie stuck by his side, offering love and encouragement, until his body gave in three years later. Alex had given her permission to move on many times, but true love didn't walk away when life got tough, and loyalty mattered to them both.

Lizzie's throat burned at the memory of hearing Alex's last breath. The following days she'd moved through the necessary motions as if lost in a dense fog.

When she finally recognized blue skies and the sun on her face, she also began to think clearly again. Lizzie would never find another love like the one she'd shared with Alex, and she would never have a family of her own. She'd avoid heartbreak and loss by creating a life for herself, and that also meant finding a way to become financially independent.

Her parents owned a restaurant in Portland. For years, she'd helped prepare food in the kitchen, and she'd also served as a waitress. But after Alex's death, Lizzie had poured her energy into the family business and its success. She learned the various aspects of running a successful establishment, including inventory and managing the books. Lizzie wasn't proficient at everything—yet—but she was learning and working hard, demonstrating her capabilities.

Then her father explained his feelings about women and business. As much as he loved his daughter, when the time came for him to step aside, Lizzie would not be deemed fitting to take his place. Her father intended to hand over the restaurant to her younger brother, Joseph, who at twenty-one still displayed little ambition. No amount of pleading her case made a difference.

Lizzie, heartbroken that her father was afraid to entrust his legacy to her after all she'd sacrificed and all the ways she'd proven herself, had made a promise to herself. No matter how long it took, she would find a way to open her own place, and she'd do it without anyone's help.

Four

L izzie stifled one yawn but another escaped. Somehow, she managed to balance the infant in one arm while covering her open mouth with her free hand. "I'm sorry."

"Didn't get much sleep last night?" Julia smiled and took the child.

"What gave that away?" Lizzie gently touched her lips to the baby's soft forehead. "Ernest woke up every two to three hours. He'd drink a small amount of milk, then go back to sleep, but I tossed and turned, listening to every little hiccup, waiting for him to rouse. As soon as I dozed off, he stirred again, needing a diaper change, another bottle, or soothing."

Julia held the child's tiny hand between her fingers. "Newborns typically don't sleep much at first, but that will change. And he's probably missing his mama."

"I'll do my best to bring her home to you, Ernest." Lizzie blinked the moisture forming in the corners of her eyes into submission. How ridiculous—getting emotional over leaving him for a short time. The baby had only been in Lizzie's care for twenty-four hours. Why was she feeling hesitant when she had complete confidence in Julia?

On her way out, Lizzie stopped at the wall mirror near the front door to Brown Hall to check for any missed spots of baby drool. All appeared presentable. The navy ribbon wrapped around the crown of her straw hat was the perfect accent to her white shirtwaist, navy skirt with a wide cloth belt, and navy jacket.

Despite the hat's protective brim, as she opened the large main door, brilliant rays from the rising sun almost blinded her.

"Good morning!"

Lizzie shielded her eyes from the glare and was surprised to see Jack Butler sitting in a buggy while his horse nibbled on the lawn. Instead of overalls and a work shirt, he was dressed in a nice-fitting suit.

He hopped out and met her at the base of the steps. She'd been so distracted by Ernest the day before, she hadn't completely taken in his lean but muscular build or his warm brown eyes that now reminded her of hot cocoa.

"Jack, what are you doing here?"

"Did the baby's mother come back for him?"

"No . . ." Why had he avoided her question? Why not just tell her why he'd shown up that morning?

He raked fingers through his dark hair. Then with one hand grasping the back of his neck, Jack studied the ground as though seeking an answer to a question not yet asked. "You going to look for her?"

"How did you know?"

"Overheard you and Helen talking in the kitchen yesterday." He gave her a sly smile. "I didn't intentionally eavesdrop. I was just doing my job—the beans, corn—you know."

"Of course." His listening to their conversation wasn't the issue. Why had he taken such an interest?

"I'd like to give you a hand—with finding the little guy's mother." He gestured toward the buggy. "I'm offering a ride to the railroad station or anywhere else you want to search, and I'll help you look for her. You never know what you might run into."

She'd only just met this man, and believing it necessary to prove her ability to handle challenges on her own, Lizzie would rather not depend on anyone for assistance.

"I understand that you don't know me well, but we are on first-name basis, and Helen will vouch for me. I also brought a comfortable buggy instead of the wagon, so hopefully that's another thing in my favor." The glint in his eyes suggested a bit of teasing in his attempt to persuade.

"All true."

He shrugged nonchalantly and grinned. "While you're trying to decide whether to trust me or not, we're wasting time that could be used to find baby Ernest's mama."

"You're right . . . and it would be quicker to take a direct route to the station as opposed to taking two or three streetcars." And the company might be pleasant as well. Jack certainly seemed like a thoughtful and compassionate man. There was no logical reason for Lizzie to hesitate further. "Thank you. I appreciate your generous offer."

℃℞

"Why is it so important to you that we find this woman? She gave the child up, why not let it go?" Maybe Jack was treading into territory that was none of his business, but he had to know if there was a connection between Lizzie and Nellie. "A friend or relative of yours?"

Lizzie's eyebrows shot up, then she glared at him with a force that could have knocked him off his seat. "What a ridiculous question. Why was it important for you to show up uninvited and offer to spend the day looking for a woman you've never met?"

Jack swallowed. "I like a good mystery." Although the truth, solving one had nothing to do with his desire to find Nellie. "And I know what it's like to grow up without a mother." He hadn't meant to share that information, but if he expected Lizzie to be up-front with him, she deserved something in return.

"I'm so sorry, Jack." Lizzie's shoulders relaxed, and her eyes softened.

"She didn't die. Mom left when my brother and I were just kids. We haven't heard from her since, and Dad raised us on his own." Jack shrugged. "I think he did a pretty good job, but it still hurts at times. As a youngster, you wonder if it was because you did something wrong."

"Jack, nothing you did or said could have caused your mother to walk away from her family. There has to be more to the story." Lizzie's tone didn't reek of admonition, only kindness, and that unexpectedly touched him. "But I understand how her absence could be painful."

"Thanks." Jack heaved a sigh. "We all did fine without her, but I sure won't be putting myself in my father's position. I watched him ache over the loss for years."

"So marriage isn't in your future?"

"No, ma'am."

"I understand." Lizzie offered a gentle smile. "It's not in mine either."

"Hmmm . . ." Maybe Jack had found a companion of sorts. Someone he could be around without fear of giving the wrong impression. He'd learned to keep his distance from marriage-seeking women.

Jack pulled back on the reins and brought the buggy to a halt as two women with a small child and a baby carriage crossed the road. When they were safely out of the buggy's path, he directed his mare to move, and the animal continued on down the road. "Enough about me. Are you willing to answer *my* question?"

"Oh, yes! Ernest's mother is a new acquaintance—a friend. Nellie sells flowers outside the train station, and when I first arrived in Seattle, she literally saved me from possible harm."

Lizzie settled back against the seat. "My brother was going to meet me at the station, but I took an earlier train than originally planned. Instead of waiting for Timothy to finish teaching for the day, I decided to surprise him. I thought I could find another way of transportation to Brown Hall, but I hadn't considered my options, and I had no knowledge of Seattle."

A mischievous smile hinted that she carried a rebellious spirit. "I'm too unfettered at times for my family's comfort, and that day my rash decision could have gotten me in trouble."

"How did Nellie come to your rescue?"

"I couldn't walk the distance to Brown Hall from the train station, even without my luggage. Carriages were lined up on the streets, ready to provide their services. A polite driver approached me, and his fee for delivering me to the orphanage seemed reasonable, so I agreed to hire him.

"Nellie saw what was happening. She warned me that it was unsafe to ride with him, and she assured me that if I was willing to wait a short time, another carriage would soon return. Intuition told me that I could trust the flower saleswoman, so I declined the shady gentleman. Angry at losing a fare, his face turned the same shade as burgundy wine. But I would have blindly gotten in and been whisked away had Nellie not grabbed me and pulled me aside."

That sounded like his Nellie—quick to save. "She was familiar with this man?"

"I won't go into the sordid details, but she'd heard enough stories at the station to believe he was dangerous. The vermin liked to brag about his conquests."

Jack's temper boiled inside as he imagined what that snake might have done to Lizzie—to any woman. "You arrived at the orphanage safely?"

"Another carriage driver returned, and Nellie promised that I could rely on him to take good care of me. She introduced us, and he was a complete gentleman." Lizzie smiled. "My brother was livid with me for being so impulsive, but his anger didn't last."

"And now she's left her baby with you? After just that short encounter?" Jack hadn't seen Nellie for years, but he couldn't imagine why she'd forsake her child.

"Nellie had been so kind to me, and I liked her. Knowing that she was alone and eight months pregnant, I visited her often at the station. I kept her company, brought meals that we shared together, and we talked. I didn't pry into her personal life, so I don't know anything about her son's father, but I'd hoped that she'd someday have enough faith in me to trust that I didn't judge her.

"I became more concerned about her health, because the last time I saw her, she looked pale and seemed a bit weak. I worried that something might be wrong, but she insisted that she was fine."

"You've been a good friend to her." Guilt weighed heavy on Jack. If he'd remained in contact, would Nellie still have given away her child, or would he have influenced her to keep and raise Ernest? And where was the father?

"What will happen to Ernest if we can't find Nellie? What kind of life will he have?" Was Lizzie talking to herself, or did she expect him to answer?

"Could it be possible that . . . ?" Jack rubbed his jaw. How could he suggest such an awful thing? "There is no positive outcome? I mean, is an orphanage the right place for any child? Like you said, what kind of life will he have if no one claims him?"

"Jack!" Lizzie sounded appalled at his suggestion. "If God is as loving as I've been taught—as compassionate as my brother insists—then there has to be something good that comes out of this for both Nellie and Ernest."

"I want to believe that." Would God still bless an act that seemed so selfish? Was that where grace and mercy applied? "I'm still having a difficult time connecting the gentle woman who went out of her way to protect you and the mother who is willing to give up her child."

"I know it doesn't make sense, but Helen reminded me that we don't know all the facts." Lizzie held on to the side of the buggy as they bounced over a small hole in the road. "Mothers—and fathers—can feel desperate, even hopeless, when they believe they're unable to care for their children. It's not that they don't love them. Sometimes, they think the only option they have to save their children is to place them in an orphanage for temporary care or adoption."

They turned onto a busier road bordered with a variety of booming businesses. Jack's awareness of carriages coming and going and pedestrians trying to maneuver their way from one side of the street to the other was imperative. It would be dangerous to become distracted, but his conversation with Lizzie was also too important to ignore.

"So, you're convinced that the baby's mother must have good reasons for what she did." He wanted to understand, but he was doing a poor job of conveying it. If he was forthcoming about his relationship to Nellie, all would become clearer to Lizzie. But how and when?

"If Ernest stays with us, he'll still be raised with love, and he'll receive an education. Brown Hall isn't like many of the other institutions. You must have seen that with your own eyes during your deliveries. It's nothing like *Oliver Twist*."

"I apologize, Lizzie." Now he felt like a cad for insinuating the orphanage might be an unacceptable situation. "You're right to correct me."

"You're also not wrong. Orphanages are often horrible places where the mortality rate isn't much better than on the streets. Older, bigger, tougher kids prey mercilessly on younger, smaller children. For some, living in an orphanage means either becoming a predator or a victim.

"But Reverend Brown and his wife with the Children's Home Society have been working for reform, and they want to place orphaned children for adoption in family foster care rather than in orphanages. Their mission is to find a home for *every* child."

"I wish them success." He smiled at her. "In the meantime, let's hope and pray we find this baby's mother and that she wants to take him back."

"You still haven't explained why you're so invested in finding Nellie."

A black open-topped Model T drove by with a distinctive low *chug-chug-chug* sound, making Shine skittish. Jack guided the animal to the side of the road in front of a drug store, where the horse calmed down. "We're all getting used to having more cars on the street. Before you know it, they'll outnumber horse-drawn carriages."

"I think automobiles are exciting." Lizzie turned to watch the car drive in the opposite direction. "Do you think you'll get one?"

"Someday. I talked to an owner last week, and he said driving a T is much like operating a tractor. So, it can't be too hard to get the hang of it."

Lizzie swung back and faced him. "Did you hear about the 'Ocean to Ocean Automobile Endurance Contest'? I read about it in the paper before moving to Seattle."

"I was at the expo on June twenty-second when the winning car crossed the finish line. Henry Ford was there to welcome the Model T No. 2 and its drivers, James Smith and Bert Scott. They said they were exhausted, but I think the crowd felt exhilarated. Anyway, that's how *I* felt."

"Would you have done it? Given the chance?" Lizzie's tone relayed both a challenge and her curiosity.

"I don't know." Jack wanted to believe he'd have the stamina to make the trip, but dreaming about the journey was different than actually experiencing it. "Can you imagine driving more than four thousand miles over muddy roads, snow-covered mountains, and fields and streams—and passing through more than four hundred communities between New York and Seattle? But they accomplished it, and the race was a great victory for Ford, as well as good publicity for his company."

"And for the expo." Lizzie grinned. "I also read that when the six cars in the race left New York, President Taft gave the starting signal from the White House." She released a contented sigh. "We sure are living in exciting times."

By changing the subject to automobiles, Jack had managed to avoid answering Lizzie's question about Nellie a second time. But he couldn't elude the truth much longer, and Lizzie deserved to know Jack's motivation for getting involved.

They arrived at the railroad station, and he directed Shine to pull the buggy into an area where they could tether the horse.

"Look! Over there." Lizzie pointed. "That's the corner where Nellie sold flowers. That's her wagon, but who is that girl?" She made her way to the ground before Jack could demonstrate his manners and assist her. Lizzie had mentioned her independence.

He caught up to her as she reached the flower wagon and before Lizzie began her inquiry. If this girl who had taken Nellie's place shared her whereabouts, Lizzie would refuse to go home without pursuing the lead immediately. No matter location or distance, Jack would insist on taking her. He couldn't allow this caring but naïve woman to venture off on her own into unknown territory. And just as important, he ached inside to find Nellie and help her in any way possible.

The salesgirl, who introduced herself as Martha, knew nothing about Nellie or where she had gone. The grower had hired Martha a few days before and told her she could work at that location. He'd also mentioned that the woman who used the flower cart before her had quit and was leaving Seattle. He must have been referring to Nellie. Regardless, Lizzie left a note for him with her address, requesting he contact her with any information regarding Nellie's location.

Lizzie and Jack spent almost two hours questioning other vendors, railroad employees, and travelers in the area. She pleaded with him to remain at the station until they found and questioned the carriage driver who had taken her to the orphanage when she first arrived in Seattle. No one knew where Nellie lived or if she'd left the city.

There was nothing left to do but return Lizzie to Brown Hall.

$$\mathcal{F}ive$$

City noises surrounded Jack and Lizzie as they rode back to the orphanage, once again passing carriages and automobiles heading in the opposite direction. As they drew closer to Brown Hall and the familiar residential area, activity slowed. Some pedestrians were engaged in conversation during their leisurely stroll, while others scurried along as though on an important pursuit.

The air's heaviness wasn't due to impending rain. Only a few wispy clouds traveled the blue sky. Could Jack break their silence and interrupt Lizzie's thoughts? They'd failed at finding Nellie, so what next? He couldn't pretend he wasn't personally invested in Ernest's future.

Jack turned toward her, still paying attention to the road out of the corner of his eye, but also trusting Shine to stay the course. "What will happen to the baby now?" he asked quietly.

"I don't know." Lizzie's eyes pooled. She wrung her hands, then folded them together in her lap, her knuckles white. "I've only been employed at the orphanage for a short time, so I still have much to learn. My brother and Helen will have more insight as to the process."

"Your brother?"

"Timothy Clark. He's a teacher at Brown Hall." Lizzie cocked her head. "He's worked at the orphanage since it opened, so I assumed you knew each other."

"We've met but only talked briefly, so I can't honestly say that I *know* him." The brother and sister didn't look anything alike, but maybe Jack should have asked if they were related after learning they had the same last name. "My father makes most of the farm's deliveries. When I've taken that job over, I've never stayed long enough at the orphanage to talk much to anyone—Helen being the exception."

"Hmmm . . ."

Jack, focused on the road again, felt her eyes on him. Sizing him up? Trying to decide what she wanted to share about her brother?

"The children love him." Pride filled her voice. "Timothy works with the boys. His primary focus is academics, but he also teaches woodworking, especially furniture making. The hope is that both boys and girls will learn practical skills. If they're never adopted, they'll need to find employment when the time comes for them to leave the orphanage."

They still had a distance to go before reaching Brown Hall, and if he slowed the mare's pace, they'd have even more time together. Jack didn't want this conversation to end too quickly. There was more to discover about this woman who had befriended Nellie. "Are you and Timothy close?"

"He's my best friend." Lizzie's tone rang with adoration.

Jack had wanted that kind of relationship with his own brother, but although they respected and loved each other, he and Adam had never shared anything too personal. "Had you always planned to join him at Brown Hall?"

"No . . ." A deep sigh followed her confession. "I'd envisioned a different map for my life." She sat up straight and smiled, though it seemed a bit forced. "How and why I came to Brown Hall is a long story."

"We have time." He grinned. "It might help occupy your mind, and I'd like to hear it."

"I wouldn't know where to start."

"Try the beginning."

She sat still for a moment then took a deep breath. "Our parents own a restaurant in Portland. While growing up, I befriended a girl next door named Flora. We were both around nine at the time. Flora was adopted out of an orphanage. Her parents were very good to her, but one day, I discovered food stashed in her room. It wasn't that I was snooping," she said, sounding a bit defensive. "My friend had asked me to retrieve a book for her, but I didn't find it on her dresser where she'd said to look. So I searched the room.

"When I asked Flora why she'd stored provisions, she broke down and cried. Then she admitted that she was terrified of not having enough to eat. She also worried that she'd do something to displease her parents, and they'd deny her meals as a punishment—something that was done at the institution where she'd lived. Flora hid food to cushion herself from hunger."

Jack had never gone hungry. He couldn't imagine living daily with that concern, but how many other children shared similar experiences to that little girl's? "Did she ever get over her fear?"

"I hope so, because it was obvious that her new mom and dad loved her and she them. But they moved away after that summer, and I never heard from her after that. Regardless, I never forgot Flora or that day."

"That incident—discovering how she was struggling— would make an impact on anyone." Jack had witnessed

Lizzie's compassion for Nellie and her son, but after hearing that story, his appreciation for Lizzie's heart grew even more. Too many of the young, pretty women he'd encountered seemed self-centered but not her.

She pointed to a small but welcoming house nestled between two maple trees in a yard filled with beautiful flower gardens. "Isn't Helen's home lovely? I'm happy for her—to have a place of her own and so close to the orphanage."

"After working long days like she does, she deserves a refuge." They'd arrive at Brown Hall in a few minutes. "Please tell me the rest of the story and how Flora influenced you."

"Oh, yes. Well, I promised to not tell her parents or mine about her anxiety, but I did talk to Timothy. He knew I was upset and cornered me in my bedroom." Her voice had hitched midsentence. Those memories had possibly stirred up strong emotions. "He liked Flora, and being a sensitive boy, it pained him to hear what she'd gone through before her adoption.

"Years went by, but Timothy didn't forget either. So, when we heard Reverend and Mrs. Brown speak at our church about the Children's Home Society and their mission, Timothy believed he felt God's nudge to act. A year ago, he left his teaching position at a prestigious school in Portland and moved here to Washington to help."

"But you didn't join him until recently."

"I was influenced by the convictions Timothy had followed, and I missed him. But at the time he moved to Seattle, my life was on a different path." She chewed her lower lip and turned away.

Jack buried his curiosity—for now. He sensed Lizzie wasn't ready or willing to discuss where that road had led. Plus, he couldn't judge. He kept his own secrets.

As quickly as she'd directed her focus elsewhere, she swung around and faced him. "Your turn. You never answered my question—the one I've asked several times."

"And that was . . . ?"

"You and your father have been delivering food to Brown Hall for more than a year—ever since the place was built. So out of all the children who have lived at the orphanage, why are you so invested in *this* baby? It's Sunday. Surely after working hard six days a week on the farm, you'd want rest. Yet, here you are, spending your entire morning searching for someone you don't even know."

Jack grasped the reins tighter and rubbed his thumb along the leather, as though he could gain courage from the warmth the friction created. Lizzie had opened up to him. Now it was his turn. She deserved an explanation.

"The truth is . . . the baby's mother . . . she isn't a stranger."

Lizzie gasped. "What?" Her eyes narrowed. "I don't understand. Why didn't you say something before?"

"I had reasons, just like you have yours for not divulging everything about your own personal story." He flinched at seeing her face flush. He wasn't trying to be mean—just stating the facts. "Lizzie, you and I just met. Time is a necessary component when developing trust. And getting there may take me longer than most. Call it a flaw or label it a strength, but it's who I am—a private person who doesn't share much of his life with anyone."

"I understand not wanting to discuss personal matters with everyone you meet, but this is quite a different matter.

Your relationship with Nellie could make all the difference in knowing how and where to find her."

"You have every right to be angry with me." Jack massaged his temple and sighed. "But I've realized that my privacy isn't as important as reuniting Nellie and Ernest. Nor is it as important as your opinion of me." Why had he confessed that? And when had he come to care what she thought? The moment he walked into the orphanage's kitchen and her warm smile gave him a sense of home like nothing he'd ever experienced before?

"My opinion?"

"I didn't want my friendship with Nellie and my interest in her son to give you any cause to wonder . . ."

"What?"

"If I'm the father." The idea sounded ridiculous after being spoken out loud. Jack hadn't seen Nellie in years, but Lizzie didn't know that because he'd kept that information from her.

They had only a block to go before reaching the orphanage. An older boy bolted across the road in front of them, Lizzie grabbed the side of the carriage, and Jack pulled back on the reins to halt their motion. He swallowed the reprimand that screamed inside at the clueless boy who continued on his way without so much as a wave or apology.

Jack didn't want to upset Lizzie more than he had already. But they could have easily trampled the pedestrian, hurting or even killing him if they'd been moving at a faster speed and Shine had been a different horse, less responsive to his surroundings or his master's touch. "Are you all right?"

Lizzie inhaled a deep breath, then she freed the air from her lungs and released her grasp on the carriage. "Yes. I'm fine." She shook her head as though in disbelief of the incident. "He came out of nowhere. Your quick reaction probably saved that boy from harm."

"I can't take any credit. My horse stopped in time without getting spooked." Jack chuckled softly as he urged the animal to continue down the road. "Now if I can get Shine to respond the same way to his encounter with the next Model T—"

"Good luck!" Lizzie offered a genuine smile, and her body visually relaxed. Then she shifted her position on the seat, and looking toward him again, her gaze locked with his. "I never would have accused you of being the baby's father. We've only just met, but I believe you're too honest to withhold that kind of information. And . . . you've shown that you care about what happens to Ernest. If he were your son, you would have claimed him from the start."

"Thanks."

"However, don't believe for even a minute that an *almost* accident is going to give you an excuse to not carry on with your explanation of how you know Nellie."

"Oh, yes . . . *that*." He hadn't mentioned Nellie in years. It might do him some good to tell someone, and Lizzie was the first person Jack had felt comfortable talking to since he and Nellie had gone their separate ways. "Brown Hall is up ahead. Would you mind if we stayed here beside the road while we have our little heart-to-heart?"

"I think that would best. Even if we remained in the buggy on the orphanage's premises, it's likely that we'd be interrupted." Lizzie folded her hands in her lap and smiled. "Perhaps you could start at the beginning."

He caught the twinkle in her eyes. So . . . she found turning things back on him amusing. *Touché, Lizzie.* "My story is somewhat similar to yours and Flora's."

"I'm listening."

"Nellie and I were close friends when we were kids. We both felt like outsiders. Nellie was teased because of her scar and limp. I once had a stutter so debilitating that when I became extremely stressed, I could barely breathe."

"I've never heard you stutter."

"I worked hard to overcome the impediment, but I still slip into stammering at times." Memories of that horrible day flooded his mind. "Some of the older, bigger boys at school were merciless, and they often targeted younger, vulnerable students. Nellie and I were no exceptions. But something fierce erupted in her when she witnessed unkindness to others, and I admired the way she tried to protect the people she cared about.

"Then one day when those bullies attacked me, she faced them, physically and verbally lashing out with all she had until I could get away. They seized the opportunity, took advantage of the situation, and groped her."

"Oh, Jack!" Lizzie's horrified expression took Jack back to the moment he realized what was happening to Nellie, and his stomach roiled.

"I didn't know what to do. I couldn't overtake them." His throat felt raw. "I've never forgiven myself for running away and leaving her alone with them. And I carry deep shame for not rescuing her when she endangered herself out of loyalty to me.

"She later forgave me, but nothing was ever the same between us. Our fractured bond didn't have enough time to heal because less than a year later, Nellie left to live with her grandmother, and I never saw or heard from her again."

"I'm so sorry, Jack."

"I owe her *now* what I failed to give her back *then*. Nellie once rescued me, and now it's my duty to safeguard her child's future."

"It seems like we're both trying to make up for things done in the past. But Jack . . ." Lizzie's voice was heavy with sadness. "Neither of us will have a say in where Ernest finds a home. We can only pray that if Nellie doesn't come for him, God will provide the right parents for Ernest."

Six

"Timothy, we must have talked to twenty people at the station today, but no one knew anything about Nellie," Lizzie whispered as she turned down the lamp next to her bed. Not finding anywhere else currently private enough to have this conversation, they'd settled in her room. Ernest lay sleeping, nestled in his basket a few feet away, so they'd keep their voices low.

"What about the new girl who took Nellie's place selling flowers?" Timothy dropped onto the empty chair she'd offered. "Couldn't she talk to her employer? He must have some information."

"I left a note for him with my address, asking him to contact me if he knew where I might find her. But if she's left Seattle, he may not have a clue." Lizzie sat on the edge of her bed.

She was grateful Ernest slept peacefully—at least for now—but how could his mother rest? Did Nellie toss and turn, grieving her loss?

"I learned something important about Jack today," Lizzie said. "Why he's been so interested in Ernest and finding Nellie. The two of them are—*were*—friends."

Timothy cocked his head and scowled. "He's not the baby's father, is he?"

"No!" Even in a hushed tone, Lizzie made it clear that her

brother's insinuation was far from the truth. "Jack hasn't seen Nellie since they were kids, but he realized from my description and hearing her full name that she was his childhood friend. They were very close at one time, and he still feels that bond and a deep sense of loyalty to her."

"And what if Nellie isn't willing or able to return and care for her child?"

"I think Jack feels strongly that it's up to him to defend Ernest and make sure that he's placed in a good home. But only after all other avenues are pursued and he's assured that Nellie isn't willing or capable of raising her child."

"So Jack just opened up and spilled his history with the baby's mother?"

"No, I asked him three times why he was so invested in the child's welfare before he revealed their relationship."

"And you?" Timothy raised one eyebrow. A sign that he already knew the answer but wanted to hear her excuse anyway. "How would you respond to the same inquiry?"

Lizzie toyed with the opal ring on her finger, twisting it as though the action would give her clarity. Alex had given her the jewelry before he died, and it often brought her comfort. "Of course I feel compelled to watch over baby Ernest because his mother left a note, asking me to take care of him. And even though I haven't known Nellie for long, I've felt nearer to her than any other friend." She shrugged. "How could that be?"

Timothy crossed his right leg and rested his calf on his left thigh. Then he leaned over and, after propping his right elbow on his raised thigh, he rubbed his jaw. "I believe that because we're spiritual beings, we sometimes feel a connection with other people that can't be explained. But it's there because God made us that way."

"I think I understand. It's like feeling you've known a person your entire life when you've only just met. I felt that kind of bond with Nellie."

"So it makes sense that out of that friendship, you'd want to honor her wishes."

"Yes, but there's more to it." Lizzie gazed out the small bedroom window at the crescent moon. "I'll never forget Flora and how her life was changed because good people adopted her. Yet, she still struggled with fear and distrust."

"Flora's horrible experiences impacted me too."

"And she's one of the reasons we're both here, dedicated to making a difference for children. But my motives aren't entirely unselfish."

A thumping sound came from the room above where some of the older boys slept, and Timothy raised his eyebrows. "I'll check on them if the noise continues."

Lizzie fingered the blue and green afghan lying next to her on the bed. "I need to find my place."

"I thought you were happy here."

"Oh, I am, for now. But what about my future? Every time I think I have a plan, my life gets disrupted again. Sometimes all I can see up ahead is a big black hole."

"When Alex died, I thought you might get lost in that empty space."

"I did too." She drew a corner of the afghan up to her cheek. The blanket, made by her mother, would be a cozy comfort during the cooler months ahead. "At first, all I could do was grieve the loss of him."

"Could you find enough purpose cooking for these orphans?"

"My time at Brown Hall has already felt rewarding, but I

need something I can call my own." Others felt the same way. Lizzie had heard many women express a desire to share valuable skills and talents, and she hoped they would all get a chance to use them.

"You seem quite determined to pursue that dream." Timothy tapped his thigh several times. "So, dear sister, please explain why it's so important to do it alone."

Why was her brother pushing so hard? He'd always been supportive of anything Lizzie wanted to try. "I want to be strong and independent, and I need to prove, if only to myself, that I can succeed."

"Wonderful qualities, to be sure. But there's nothing wrong with leaning on another person from time to time or asking for help."

He was becoming a bit irritating, and in doing so, he fanned a slow burn within Lizzie. "I know. And I have done just that. But there are times—"

"When your stubborn pride gets in the way." Timothy raised his arm in front of his face as though defending himself from an impending blow, but Lizzie didn't miss the impish grin nor the twinkle in his hazel eyes. There was the brother she knew and loved. He was only being difficult because he wanted Lizzie to think everything through and act on logic instead of impulse and emotion. He kept her grounded and focused.

"Yes." Lizzie gave in to her own smile, but she sobered quickly. "And now I'm conflicted because I feel drawn to Ernest and his needs. If Nellie doesn't return for him, I won't have any choice but to see him placed in another woman's arms."

"Any chance of you adopting him?"

"He deserves two parents."

"You might find someone to love again. You're a smart, sensitive, attractive woman, even if you are my sister," Timothy said with a familiar teasing tone.

"That's not likely. After Alex . . . I don't think I'll ever give my heart to another man. It's too painful to lose someone you love that much." Lizzie had healed from the deepest part of her grief, but the pain never disappeared completely. Even now, a dull ache squeezed her heart. She didn't want a heavy cloud following her or dampening anyone else's moods. Most of the time, she kept her sorrow to herself and focused on bringing a cheerful presence. She was doing a horrible job of that now.

Perhaps if she changed the subject . . . Lizzie grinned and placed a hand on his. "But you and Julia make quite a couple. How serious are you two?"

Her brother rewarded her with a deep belly laugh, stirring the baby.

"Shhh . . ." Lizzie smiled then wagged her finger at Timothy. "If you wake Ernest, you're putting him back to sleep."

He held his palms up as if surrendering to her threat. Then he settled back in the chair. "I haven't told her yet, but I love her, Lizzie. Julia is sweet and kind and gentle . . ." As Timothy spoke, his eyes softened. Yes, her brother was smitten.

"She's lovely. I'm happy for you."

"I want that for you too. You deserve to find someone who will love you and be a partner in all things—like what our parents have shared. I know Father hurt you when he made the decision to let Joseph take over the restaurant, but in reality, he doesn't discount your contributions to the business."

"Then why?"

"I can't answer for him. Maybe Father made a mistake in not choosing you. Maybe you're at the orphanage for a season because you're needed here." Timothy took his sister's hands in his. "But I do believe that God wants what's best for you, Lizzie. Can you trust that? Even if you can't see it?"

She tightened her grip. "I'm trying."

"Even if God's plan includes letting go of the past and opening up your heart to another man?"

Seven

Lizzie yawned and blinked her eyes, attempting to clear her blurry vision. The large pot of oatmeal sitting on the counter came back into focus.

"You sound a bit weary." Helen carried a kettle of boiled eggs to the sink and drained the water.

"Exhausted. Three nights of interrupted sleep." Lizzie plopped hot cereal into a small bowl, then placed it on a tray with additional servings. Now a pinch of brown sugar and a splash of milk in each portion. "How do mothers of newborns carry on like this night after night?"

Helen smiled. "I never had children of my own, so I can't speak from experience, but I've been told it gets easier. Babies eventually sleep through the night."

"Hmmm . . ." Lizzie brushed hair from her eyes, then hefted the filled tray and set it on the cart for two older girls to wheel into the dining area. They'd serve the children settling in for breakfast.

"You may not have to go without sleep much longer. Now that Ernest is spending his days in the nursery, he might soon occupy a crib there at night as well."

Helen filled a large porcelain bowl with boiled eggs and set it on the counter for delivery to the dining room. Lizzie had once suggested they peel the eggs before serving them, but Helen believed it was important for even the younger children to learn how to fend for themselves.

"More rest sounds lovely, but even though I've complained about some fatigue, I'm not ready to see Ernest move into the nursery full time. I'll miss him." Lizzie moved the empty pot to the sink. "The boys in Timothy's woodworking class are building a crib for Ernest. Maybe I'll ask my brother to build another to keep in my room."

Helen wiped her hands on a towel and gave Lizzie a sympathetic glance. "Be careful. You've been a blessing to that sweet child, but try not to get too attached. A permanent home may be found for Ernest at any time, and if he's adopted, you'll have to say goodbye. I'd hate to see your heart broken."

"I know. But I still can't give up hope that Nellie will return for him."

"We can only do our part to help these little ones and then trust God to do what's best."

"You sound like my brother. Timothy has tremendous faith in God's plans." Lizzie lifted the cloth cover that hid rising dough. "You must have started food prep early this morning."

"I woke up and couldn't get back to sleep. Emma used the water closet and heard me rustling around in here, so she came in and helped mix and knead today's batch. That girl is a treasure." Helen checked the already hot oven and set the first loaf inside. "Some people think we'll be using electricity instead of gas to heat our stoves and ovens in the future, but I'm not convinced."

"Timothy seems to agree. Inventors continually come up with creative devices to make our lives easier, don't they? We're living in exciting times with electricity, automobiles

. . . and even a world's fair right here in our city." Lizzie carried a tin with bread dough to the oven and placed it inside with the other three Helen had set there. "I can imagine there are all kinds of new gadgets displayed at the expo."

"You'll soon see for yourself." Helen closed the oven door with a smile.

Emma breezed in and surveyed the kitchen. "The children are served, and everything is under control in the dining room. What can I do to help prepare lunch?"

Lizzie caught Helen's eye, and they both chuckled.

"What?" Emma's glance ricocheted between Lizzie and Helen. "What did I say that was so funny?"

"Not funny, Emma—endearing." Helen wrapped her arm around the girl's shoulders and gave her a quick side squeeze. "I hope you know you're appreciated."

Emma's cheeks turned a shade of pink that rivaled cherry blossoms in the spring. "Thank you."

"As for lunch, we'll keep it simple with chicken sandwiches and potato salad. They had boiled eggs for breakfast, but we have plenty, as well as an abundance of cooked potatoes, cooled and ready to be sliced." Helen's hands perched on her hips. "It's hard to fill the stomachs of those growing boys. When the rest of the apples are harvested from the trees in the backyard, we'll can applesauce and store some for winter."

"Could we also bake some pies?" Emma sounded hopeful.

Lizzie nodded and smiled. "That would be a nice surprise for the children." She'd certainly enjoy the dessert as well.

"I think we might find time, if we can afford the sugar." Helen leaned against the counter.

"I know it's essential to provide meals that will help the children grow strong and healthy, but surely it's also important that they enjoy a little treat now and then. I'll pay for the sugar myself, if needed," Lizzie said, now determined to make those pies.

"Thank you. That's very generous." Helen pushed fallen strands of gray hair back from her forehead. "We'll be doing some baking then, and hopefully, I won't have to take you up on your offer."

Lizzie winked at Emma, and the girl shot her an enthusiastic grin.

"You two are obviously pleased." Shaking her head, Helen chuckled under her breath. She pulled a bin of cold, boiled eggs from the icebox and set it on the table in the middle of the kitchen.

"I can peel." Lizzie grabbed a small container for the shells.

"Thank you." Helen picked up an egg and held it in the palm of her hand. "You know, we may cook for the little ones, but other kinds of nourishment are just as important—sometimes more so."

Emma pulled a knife from a drawer and began cutting up potatoes for the salad. "By other kinds, you mean . . ."

Helen replaced the egg. "Love and attention. A smile. Genuine interest in them. Orphans have their own aspirations, and they want to believe their dreams can come true. Everyone needs a little hope to get by." She withdrew a large white ceramic mixing bowl from a cupboard and placed it where the women could add all the ingredients together.

They worked in silence, and Lizzie thought about Helen's wise words. Lizzie could do better. She had her favorites—those she sought out because they were sweet, funny, or bright. But what about those who were shy, a bit strange, or even angry? Perhaps they were merely afraid or lonely. She hadn't shown them as much kindness as the others, but that was going to change. *Lord, I've been so blind and consumed in myself. Thank you for opening my eyes.*

"Oh! I almost forgot!" Emma laid her knife down and wiped her hands on her apron. "Helen, I was asked to give you this letter. It was delivered with the mail this morning." Emma pulled an envelope from her apron pocket and handed it to the head cook.

She took the letter, slit it open with a knife, and then sat on a chair while she read silently to herself. Lizzie tried not to appear overly interested, but she watched Helen as a slow, delighted smile grew on her face.

"Good news?" Lizzie asked.

"More than good. My nephew and his wife are coming for a visit." Helen folded the letter and laid it in her lap. "Sometimes God blesses you in the most unexpected ways."

"You must be close to your nephew," Emma said, resuming her potato slicing.

"Our faith binds us together." Helen's eyes sparkled. "As a young man, my husband left the Midwest to work on the railroad. His brother took a different path and stayed on the family farm, and the two didn't communicate much after that.

"When John died, I wrote my nephew, Peter, to let him know that his uncle had passed. I've never met him or my niece, Ellie, who now has a family of her own. But we started corresponding. And now Peter and his wife, Sarah, are coming for a visit all the way from Riverton, Wisconsin, to see me and attend the expo. They plan to stay for at least a week."

"Oh, how wonderful for you," Lizzie said.

"Of course I'll insist that they stay at my place. I have a comfortable guest room. Hotels can be expensive, and with so many visitors attending the fair, it's difficult to find accommodations right now."

Helen and her husband had lived together in their small home two blocks from here until his death a short time prior to the purchase of the orphanage property by the Children's Home Society. She was seeking a way through her grief, and since she had prior experience working in a hotel restaurant, Helen applied for the head cook position at Brown Hall.

But she'd never mentioned having any additional family. Now, she would have an opportunity to spend time with her nephew and his wife, which made Lizzie genuinely happy for her friend.

Lizzie cracked and peeled another egg, then held it, lost in thought. She'd never met the couple, so what was this excitement stirring inside of her? Why did she sense adventure ahead? Did it relate to Helen? To Ernest? Or to herself?

Eight

J ack washed and rinsed the last dirty plate and laid it on a towel to dry. His father would take his turn at cooking and cleaning up after supper tomorrow night, but for now, he sat at the kitchen table having his second cup of coffee after downing the ham, fried potatoes, and green beans Jack had served proudly.

It felt like a huge accomplishment to prepare a meal and not burn it. Jack couldn't imagine making enough food to serve all those kids at the orphanage, and with contemplating that huge task, his admiration for Helen and Lizzie heightened.

His father reached for the last sugar cookie on the plate. "I was thinking today about the nice time we had at the expo when it first opened. We need to get back there as often as we can before it closes. Few people get the opportunity to have a world's fair in their backyard."

"Lots to keep up with on the farm right now with harvesting and selling crops, but you're right. I don't want to have any regrets when the expo comes to an end."

"It's sure an interesting place—all the people, entertainment, and exhibits." His father chomped his cookie, then wiped crumbs from his lips. "One thing I'll never understand. Why the Agriculture Building added a clam display. Didn't make sense to me, so I looked up the definition of *agriculture* in that dictionary of yours. It's the science or practice of farming that includes growing crops and rearing animals to provide food, wool, and other products. So tell me how those shell creatures fit in."

Jack chuckled. "Try viewing it from this perspective. Clams are harvested, just like other food sources, and the ocean is considered a field."

"Huh." His father gulped some coffee then set his cup down. "Never looked at it that way, but it makes sense."

Dishes done, Jack emptied the remaining coffee into his own cup, then rinsed the pot and set it back on the stove to wait until the next brew. Dad seemed relaxed and in the mood for talking. Maybe tonight he'd be more receptive to expanding their business.

"I was thinking the next time we plan to attend the fair, we could invite Adam and Rose to come stay for a few days and go with us."

"Sure." Jack sat in his chair and leaned back. "The expo is open until mid-October, so we still have almost seven weeks. Plenty of time to take in the sights again—more than once if we choose to." He eyed his father. "You might consider asking Helen to go with you. I believe she's a little sweet on you."

"Nah, she couldn't be." By the way his father's lips twitched, fighting a smile, it was obvious he was pleased by the possibility. "Helen's a kind person who's nice to everyone who walks through the door."

"That she is, but if I were a betting man, I'd make a wager that she'd gladly accept an invitation from you."

Until a few minutes ago, Jack hadn't considered the pairing of the two. Why hadn't he seen it before? Helen and his father must be about the same age—fifty-something, and they'd make an attractive couple. Although his father had grayed, physical farm work had kept him lean and muscular.

"I'll give it some thought." He pointed to the folded *Seattle Star* lying on the table. "I read that by the time the expo closes, the number of visitors will have reached the millions. Think about it, Jack. What the fair's success can accomplish for our city—our state. And what it will do for your brother's alma mater . . . well, I can't even imagine all the benefits. But with the expo being held on the University of Washington's campus, the school will inherit some of the buildings and gardens."

Jack cringed inside, but he nodded. His father was proud of Adam, and so was Jack, but he still suffered moments of envy toward his younger brother.

"I sometimes think about that day back in June when the guards thought they saw smoke coming from the roof of the Agriculture Building. But when the firefighters arrived, they discovered it was only a giant cloud of gnats." Jack's father guffawed. "And then a resident from Yakima claimed his town beat out Wenatchee as home of the Washington apple. That sure caused a ruckus."

"The expo has everyone's interest now, but in a couple of months, people's lives are going to get back to normal." Jack tightened his grip on his cup, and he cleared his throat. He'd tried broaching the subject before, and his father had disagreed, but Jack wasn't ready to give up. "And when they do, I want to talk more about applying for a spot at the Pike Place Market. We need to submit our application if we want to get accepted for the spring opening."

His father sighed. "Jack . . . the business is already doing well enough. We get by just fine."

"That might be true, but what's stopping us from building on what we have?"

"Why add more work to our load? I'm not getting any younger, and to sell more produce, we'd have to grow more. Where would we do that?"

"I'd like to offer Ed Warner a deal on some acreage. It's good land, and he's mentioned that at his age and with no sons to take over the farm, he won't continue much longer."

"Why are you set on peddling at the market?"

"Maybe if you saw what it's like to sell and shop there . . ." How many times had Jack tried to convince his father to go with him? "It's a fantastic opportunity to offer crops directly to local shoppers instead of to middlemen or the wholesale commission houses. Farmers make more money, and customers are able to feed families on their limited incomes."

"The idea sounds good, but I still have doubts that the market's popularity will last."

Why did his father have to be so stubborn? "My plan isn't as big of a gamble as you think, Dad. Pike Place Market has been open for two years, so it's a proven success."

"And you would define its glowing achievements as what?"

"You can't dispute that over a hundred farmers sell out there daily, and thousands of shoppers visit. It's in a great location with access to the trolleys. The sidewalks are covered to keep people out of the rain, so even the weather isn't a deterrent to the open market." Would Dad finally understand that the opportunity could be the gateway for Jack to achieve his own dreams?

A slow, knowing smile grew on his father's face, and he nodded. "All right. You've got a fire lit inside of you. I'll give your ideas of expanding some serious thought—and prayer."

"Thanks, Dad." This wasn't the first time he'd broached the idea of building their business. Why was his father willing to consider it now? Had Jack made a better case for his proposal? Or was something else going on? Whatever the reason, he wouldn't push any harder now and jeopardize the progress made that night.

"Chores are finished, and it will still be light for several hours, so I'm heading to Brown Hall with a delivery."

"What's up?" Dad rapped his fingers on the table, a habit when thinking. "Tomorrow is Thursday. Deliveries aren't until Saturday."

"I picked raspberries and wild blackberries earlier today. They might be a nice surprise for the kids in the morning. Heaven knows, those wild bushes are going to take over the south side of the farm before we know it."

His father's eyes twinkled with mischief. "Any other reason you want to spend time at the orphanage?"

Jack nodded. "I want to check on Ernest."

"I know you're feeling a certain responsibility to Nellie's child, but I've wondered if you might also be interested in Lizzie. I've met the gal, and she's not only pretty, she's kind."

"I have no intention of getting involved with any woman—and you've known that for a long time."

"Don't miss out on a loving relationship and the chance to have your own family because of what your mother did."

"You're a stronger man than I am." Jack leaned back in his chair and crossed his arms. "I can't forget."

"I may not be vocal about my faith, but it's what helped me deal with the pain. It's what got me through." His father stretched forward and rested his arms on the table, still clutching his coffee cup. He tapped the mug several times on the table's surface as if to make sure Jack was paying attention. "Forgive her, Son. There's a lot you don't know. Your mother was hurting. I thought I could help. I tried to make everything all right, but I couldn't, so it feels like I failed her."

"You're not at fault."

"It was hard on you boys—on me too."

"I was only ten. Adam—six. All the nights that Adam cried himself to sleep, not understanding where or why . . ." Jack shook his head. "And now Nellie—someone I used to trust—has also abandoned her child. How does a mother do that? Doesn't she think about how her son will feel as he grows older? The questions that will never be answered?"

His father pushed back his chair from the table and stood, then he grabbed the paper in one hand and his cup in the other. "We don't know what Nellie has experienced—*is* experiencing. The pain she may be bearing. And the same goes for your mother. You've never heard the entire story."

"How could I? You've never been willing to talk about what happened."

"No, I haven't, and you have a right to know." His father's eyes glistened with sorrow. "But I can't start that discussion now—not tonight."

Jack was a grown man. What reason could there be for denying him the truth? What could be so horrific that his father couldn't bring himself to share the full story of why Jack's mother had left?

Nine

J ack considered pulling up to the front of Brown Hall, hiking up the steps and between the tall white pillars, then crossing the wide porch and knocking on the front door merely because he'd never walked through the front entrance. But to deliver the heavy boxes loaded with berries, it made more sense to guide his horse around to the back where he could enter the kitchen directly.

Children filled the side yard, playing in the bright, warm, August evening. Two boys tossed a ball back and forth, but others were engaged in games like tag, hide-and-seek, hop-scotch, London Bridge, duck-duck-goose, and follow-the-leader.

"Whoa, Shine," Jack said as he pulled on the reins. He stopped next to two girls of about eight years of age jumping rope. "Would you please let Miss Clark know that Mr. Butler is here?"

The girl with a blue bow in her long blond hair nodded, dropped the rope, and raced toward the kitchen door with her red-headed jumping partner close behind.

Jack tied Shine to a post and hefted two large crates of berries into his arms. It had taken him almost three hours to pick the fruit, but it was worth it to surprise the children.

Dressed in an apron, Lizzie swung open the screen door as he reached the steps, and she met his grin with one of her own. "What are you doing here, Jack?"

For an instant, his focus dropped to the gift he carried. "Raspberries and blackberries. I thought the kids would enjoy them for breakfast."

"Oh! How thoughtful." Lizzie held the door open, but stepped aside, giving him room to enter the kitchen. She wiped her hands on her apron, then gestured toward the large, empty table. "Helen and I just finished cleaning the kitchen. You can put them there."

He set the crates down.

"Thank you!" Helen's fingers skimmed the berries, then she picked out three and popped them in her mouth. "Sweet and delicious. The children will be delighted."

Lizzie untied and slipped off her apron, then she placed it on a hook. "I have no doubt that despite how generous you and your father are with all of the orphans, this visit is an excuse to see Ernest," she said with a hint of teasing. "I was about to give him a bottle."

"I didn't mean to intrude." Jack shouldn't take more of their time. Lizzie had enough to take care of without him showing up unexpectedly, and Ernest was only a baby. He wouldn't know if Jack was there or not and neither would Nellie. "I should be going."

"There's no reason for you to come all this way and then leave without seeing him. It doesn't matter how much attention he gets from me or anyone else, a child can always use more people interested in his well-being." Lizzie pulled a chair away from the table. "Here. Please sit and wait for me. I'll only be a minute."

"Hi, Jack!" Emma said, entering the kitchen. She took two bottles of milk from a kettle on the stove. "I'm helping in the nursery tonight, and the little ones are hungry! I'm surprised you can't hear them wailing in here." She tipped one bottle at a time until milk dribbled onto her wrist. "Perfect temperature." Emma left with sustenance in hand.

"Would you like a glass of water? Cup of tea?"

"Neither. I'm fine. Thanks, Helen."

"You're welcome." She poured the steaming drink into a blue cup for herself. "Lizzie can't seem to give up Ernest's care to those in charge of the nursery. She's still keeping him in her room at night, and she checks on him every free minute of the day. You have nothing to worry about regarding the amount of attention that baby gets. My only concern is that Lizzie is getting so attached, she'll be heartbroken when the time comes to say goodbye."

Lizzie returned with Ernest cradled in her arms. "This boy is the sweetest baby. I do believe he's the favorite in the nursery." She accepted a bottle from Helen, then sat in a chair next to Jack where he could watch Ernest consume the warm nourishment, his soft whimpers now silenced.

A woman strode into the kitchen as though on a quest. Her dark and white strands of hair equally mixed were severely pulled back and pinned up, and her piercing eyes were the shade of black walnuts. Jack had seen her from a distance when making deliveries, and he guessed her to be about fifty. "Excuse me. I didn't mean to interrupt."

Helen smiled. "You're not interrupting a thing."

"I thought I might make some tea," the newcomer said, surveying Jack.

"You're welcome to the hot chamomile in the blue china pot next to the stove." Helen sipped her portion of the brew. "And I just filled the sugar bowl, if you'd like to add any."

"Thank you. That will save me some time." The woman filled a matching cup to Helen's. "I'll take it with me and get back to grading papers." She gave Jack another once-over.

"Forgive my poor manners." Helen set her drink on the table. "Cora, this is Jack Butler. He and his father provide the orphanage with fruits and vegetables. Jack, please meet Miss Cora Harper, one of the instructors here at Brown Hall. While Lizzie's brother, Timothy, oversees curriculum for the boys, Miss Harper focuses on classes for our girls."

Jack stood and nodded to the woman. "Nice to meet you, Miss Harper."

"Likewise, Mr. Butler." She leaned over Lizzie's shoulder and peered at Ernest, her expression softening. "Poor child to be abandoned like he was, but it's a blessing he was left at *this* orphanage and not one of the others. The children are well cared for here."

"Have you always been an educator, Miss Harper?" Jack asked. Teachers weren't allowed to be married, and since Helen had introduced her as *Miss* Harper . . .

"Yes, I originally taught in public schools, but I left my last position when Reverend Brown asked me to consider teaching at Brown Hall." Her mood seemed to lighten, and she offered a hint of a smile, but it was enough for Jack to catch it. "I felt it my Christian duty to provide education for the girls here and mentor them toward leading productive, godly lives."

"And you do a wonderful job." Lizzie smiled. "They're fortunate to have such a dedicated teacher."

"I sincerely work hard." Miss Harper had returned to a more serious tone. "God only knows what would have become of the children placed here without Reverend and Mrs.

Brown's passion for reform. They're doing all they can for them."

"I see these children every week, but I realize I don't have much knowledge about what actually takes place here." Until meeting Lizzie and getting involved with Ernest, Jack had been more focused on his own business as opposed to learning about the orphans' plight.

Miss Harper eyed him, but Jack couldn't discern what she felt about his confession. "You're not alone. For instance, not many know that several months ago, seventeen children were relinquished for permanent care to the Washington Children's Home Society from the Black Diamond and Roslyn coal-mining districts."

"That many? At the same time?" Jack stepped back, stunned. How could any organization deal with that number all at once?

She nodded. "Some came from homes described as extremely unfortunate, but if I recall correctly, the group included three malnourished infants, one overworked 'little sister mother,' and youngsters who were considered as on their way to a life of crime. Fifteen of those children have been placed in adoptive homes."

Jack glanced at Lizzie. Those beautiful green eyes studied him. Waiting to see how he'd respond to the information? He had no words.

The passionate teacher replenished her cup. "I must get back to work. Thank you again for the tea, Helen." She slipped out of the room as quickly as she'd come in.

Lizzie set the baby's empty bottle on the table, lifted Ernest to her shoulder, and patted him gently on his back. She gave Jack a slight smile. "Miss Harper is quite a force, isn't she?"

"If I were her student, I'd be scared to step out of line." Jack wiped his brow and returned to his seat. "I imagine she doesn't take kindly to any shenanigans."

"She can be harsh, but I believe there's a soft heart beneath that cool exterior. She's certainly dedicated to her students." Lizzie patted Ernest three more times, and he let out a quiet burp.

"Cora has mentioned not marrying because she could never give up teaching, but I believe there was a suitor years ago." Helen sipped her tea. "But of course, to talk about that would be gossip, so we won't." She rose and set her empty cup on the counter. "I'd like to finish reading my book before bed, so I'll retire to my room."

"A romance novel?" Lizzie asked.

Helen chuckled. "Oh, heavens, no. A mystery." She gave a brief wave. "Good night, you two."

After Helen left, Lizzie smiled at Jack, and her eyes twinkled. "Here, you take him."

Before Jack knew it, she'd placed Ernest in his arms. "I don't know how to hold a baby."

"Really?" She raised her eyebrows, and her eyes shone with amusement. "You haven't dropped him yet."

"He does fit well here."

"Like he belongs," she said softly.

"What do I do now?"

"Just hold him close and rock." Lizzie, pretending to cradle a newborn, swayed slowly.

How to describe what Jack felt in that moment—protective, yes—but something else melted in his heart. He stroked the boy's soft cheek, hoping his rough finger didn't irritate the baby's delicate skin. The infant's eyelids slowly closed until his long dark lashes touched his face. "It's been five days since Ernest was brought here and five days without a word from Nellie. She's not coming back for him, is she?"

"We don't know that." Lizzie's response declared some truth, but the sadness in her tone relayed her doubt.

"I don't understand how any mother could walk away from her child. It's so completely selfish." Jack kept his voice low so he wouldn't wake Ernest, but he still couldn't hide the anger.

"Try not to judge too harshly. Nellie may have had good reasons for leaving Ernest with us. She may have felt she had no other option. Women don't have many choices—at least, they're not given the same opportunities as men."

"You're right." Jack knew nothing about Nellie's circumstances. "We don't have any facts behind her decision."

"Maybe in time, some things will change for women. Right now, we don't even have the right to vote in Washington State." She grimaced. "Because of bias, women are sometimes treated as though we're less intelligent than men."

"*Some* people are working hard toward a shift." Shame at neglecting the cause nudged his conscience. He'd be more vocal from now on. "Did you know the suffrage movement was celebrated at the expo with its own day in July? Hundreds of women were in the city attending a national convention, and they rallied at the fair."

"Yes! And now the state legislature has scheduled a referendum on women's voting rights for next year."

Ernest stirred, stretched out his arms, and wailed. Jack stood and holding him close, paced the kitchen floor, trying to soothe the crying baby. He was about to give up and return the child to Lizzie, but Ernest calmed.

Jack hadn't missed the passion in her voice when she'd spoken about the suffrage movement, but there was something else going on in her head—her heart. "I know I can't completely understand what you've experienced, but I also don't think frustration over not having the right to vote is the whole story. What *aren't* you saying?"

She sat quietly, thinking for a moment, and then she sighed. "As a woman, I don't have the same advantages as my brothers." Her brows furrowed, and she moistened her bottom lip. "I worked hard to learn as much as I could about our family's restaurant, hoping to take it over one day. My father loves me, but like many men, he doesn't believe women are capable of running a business."

"He wouldn't give you a chance?"

"My father made it clear that he would never change his mind as long as I remain unmarried."

"I see." Jack didn't miss the emotional hitch in her voice. "You're a kind and intelligent woman. I can imagine many suitors vying for your attention." Why was he waiting in anticipation of her answer? Why was it so important that he know if Lizzie was involved with a man?"

"No . . . there has been no one special in a long time."

"But there *was* someone?"

"My fiancé. But Alex became very ill, and although he fought hard to stay with me, he lost the final battle."

"I'm sorry." Was it appropriate to ask questions? Comfort her? Should he even try? "You must have loved him a great deal."

Lizzie nodded. "Deeply." Her eyes relayed the grief she still carried. "We met as children and were almost inseparable, so I feel his absence every day." She offered a hint of a smile. "But I try to focus on happy memories and be grateful for what we shared."

"I admire your strength." Jack had never cared that much

for any woman. He'd never allowed himself to even consider a close relationship. A wife would deserve a part of him he wasn't willing to surrender.

"My father doesn't understand my motivation for living independently, and he sees no reason for me not to be just like my mother." Lizzie raised her hands and then dropped them. "She's always supported his accomplishments, but she's also been content focusing on gardening and her church activities. Because Timothy has no interest in the restaurant, my younger brother will inherit the business."

"It doesn't feel fair. I understand that." The baby's eyes were closed, and his chest moved up and down in small, rhythmic breaths. Jack moved back to his chair and sat with one smooth action.

"Perhaps—perhaps, it's not a matter of whether we're male or female, but circumstances. Or whether God has something else in store for us and we just can't see it at the time. I keep hoping that's the case for myself." Lizzie's eyes held a sweet fondness as she gazed at Ernest. "I'm still going to find a way to open a restaurant or a small café—a place where I can serve good food—make people feel comfortable and at home."

"Even though men have more freedom than women, not all are destined to lead lives of their choosing. Some give up their dreams out of duty, responsibility, or loyalty."

"Is that what you've done, Jack? Given up on what you wanted for *your* life?" she asked quietly, her eyes filled with compassion.

Could he try to explain? He trusted Lizzie, and it wasn't like she was going to put anything he shared in the newspaper. "As a boy, I wanted to leave the farm—venture out—explore. Like you, create something of my own. Maybe build a successful business out of nothing. You know . . . test myself and see what I could do with some inspiration, gumption, and hard work."

"What happened?"

"My younger brother, Adam, is smart. He always had his nose in books. About the time I was going to leave farming and try something different, Adam was accepted into veterinary school at the university here. My dad needed help running the farm, so I stayed."

"And your brother?"

"He's happy working as a vet for farmers up north, and he married the perfect woman for him." Jack shrugged his shoulders. "It's not that I don't enjoy farming—I do. But I'm working to continue my father's dream. He isn't interested in doing anything differently than what he's done for years."

"But you have ideas for changes?"

Jack nodded. "But I can't make them without his approval. That's the problem. How do I convince him to let me take the reins?"

Ten

"**N**o! This is pure insanity! Ernest is a child, not a trinket to be won by a fairgoer. Even if giving him away at the expo draws attention to the orphanage, it's a horrifying act." Lizzie, her stomach knotted in pain, spat out her words as she paced the kitchen floor.

"I'm sorry, Lizzie, but it's not against the law, and everything has already been put into motion. The facts are right here in the *Seattle Star*—in black and white." Helen sniffed and wiped moisture from her cheek. "We can only pray for the best outcome," she said, withdrawing a handkerchief from a pocket.

Lizzie's head ached, as though a hammer beat the inside of her skull, and her heart felt like it was being shredded. She glanced at Julia, who had retrieved Ernest from the nursery and held him within sight. Intuitive, she must have known Lizzie would need the baby close, now more than ever. "Timothy, is there *anything* we can do?"

Her brother, covered in sawdust, wrapped his arms around Lizzie, and she clung to him, inhaling the cedar scent. He was in the woodworking shop when Julia informed him earlier of the decision made by L. J. Covington, the state superintendent of Children's Home Society.

"I'm sorry, but Reverend Brown and I tried convincing Covington to withdraw from Exhibitor's Day when we reached him by phone this morning. He's gotten approval from the board, and he's going ahead with the raffle."

A burning smell crawled into the room. "Oh, dear!" Helen scrambled to grab towels before she flung open the oven door. Heavier smoke billowed around her as she pulled bread from the interior, the tops now black instead of golden brown.

Helen slammed the oven door and wiped her brow. "Goodness! I haven't ruined any food in ages, but I completely forgot about the loaves baking."

"Don't blame yourself. We're all pretty shook up," Julia said.

Someone rapped on the screen door. "Hello!" The door squeaked open. "Is something on fire?"

Hearing Jack's voice behind her, Lizzie withdrew from Timothy's arms, and as soon her gaze met Jack's, she melted into an emotional puddle. "Nothing is more ablaze in here than my temper at the moment." Her eyes prickled, and her vision blurred as she stood with hands clenched to her sides.

Helen waved at the smoky air with a towel. "Burned bread is the least of our woes. We're all upset about Ernest."

Jack dropped a large bag of potatoes on the floor and stepped farther into the room. "He's all right, isn't he?"

"He's being raffled at the expo!" Lizzie said, forcing the disgusting words into existence.

Jack's eyes narrowed. "If you're playing a joke on me, this isn't funny."

"We're not." Timothy drew Lizzie to his side. "I wouldn't call it a lottery, but Ernest is considered the prize."

"Someone better explain what's going on," Jack said in a demanding tone.

The baby started to fuss in Julia's arms, and she put her

hand on Lizzie's shoulder. "I'll take him to the nursery and put him down for a nap."

"Thank you." Lizzie felt lightheaded, and she wanted to curl up under a shade tree and escape from more heartbreak.

"I've had the ovens on for hours, and the air in here is stifling," Helen said. "Instead of remaining in this sweltering room, let's talk outside. We can sit at the table under the maple tree. No one will bother us, and it might do us all good to get some fresh air."

"I just want some answers." Jack sounded agitated.

"Timothy, there's lemonade in the icebox." Helen removed glasses from a cabinet and placed them on a tray. "Would you please carry the pitcher outside for me?"

"Yes, of course." He released his sheltering hold on Lizzie and retrieved a large container filled with the citrus drink. He also grabbed the copy of the *Seattle Star* lying on the table.

No classes were held on Saturday, so under supervision, children played freely in the large yard. They must have sensed the adults' demeanor, because no child approached Helen, Jack, Lizzie, or Timothy with any requests or questions. The four adults settled in at the table outside, and Helen poured each a glass of refreshment.

"Now, will someone please explain what's going on?" Jack shoved a hand back through his hair. "What's this about Ernest being raffled?"

Timothy handed him the newspaper. "You can read it for yourself, but it won't tell you anything more. Someone from the board should have warned us, but we didn't know anything until the paper arrived this morning. Then I made some calls and confirmed the report."

Tears pooled in Lizzie's eyes as her resilience weakened,

and she attempted to clear her raw throat. "Sunday, September nineteenth, has been designated as Exhibitor's Day at the expo. The paper states that a total of seventy-five thousand prizes will be given away. Some will be small—like an apple or a bar of soap. Others . . ." She gulped a sob. "Others will be much more significant—like a baby."

Jack's face turned the shade of fresh blood. "Who came up with this crazy idea?"

"Let me give it to you from the source." Timothy picked up the newspaper. "'The Children's Home Society said they will raffle off one of the six babies they have to be adopted.'" He took a deep breath. "The superintendent, L. J. Covington from Washington Children's Home Society, gave this statement. 'We believe we should participate in the giveaway at the fair.'"

Lizzie caught Jack's gaze with hers, and the pain she witnessed sent another wave of grief through her. "Exhibitor's Day is only a week away, and Ernest will be a month old. Covington believes that an infant will draw more attention to the Children's Home Society."

Jack raised his arms with an air of frustration. "The prize is Nellie's son!"

"Yes, and apparently, it's not the first time something like this has been done." Timothy blew air from his lungs. "I was informed today that in an effort to raise money and find homes for orphaned children, a Paris foundling hospital held a raffle of live babies. The children found homes, and proceeds were divided among several charitable institutions. Those responsible believed everyone benefited, including the orphans. Fortunately, the winners were investigated to make sure they would be desirable parents."

"So it's not *entirely* bad news." Helen's focus shifted until she'd looked all three of them in the eyes. "Ernest *could* be adopted by wonderful parents—or he might not be adopted at all by anyone attending the fair."

"People won't be buying tickets with the objective of winning a baby." Timothy refilled his glass with lemonade, but without taking a drink, he set it aside and shook his head. Because the entire idea of raffling off a child turned his stomach or because he struggled to believe in what the newspaper stated?

He glanced around the table, his eyes filled with concern. "Everyone who enters the expo that day will have a prize number printed on their stub. They'll all win *something* from an exhibit, but they won't know what they'll receive until they match up their numbers inside the entrance."

"But similar to the raffle in Paris," Lizzie added, "Covington has stated that adopting Ernest is contingent on the winner actually wanting to adopt and meeting the qualifications required by the orphanage."

A large ant crawled up the side of her glass, heading for a swim. She didn't care enough to brush the insect aside. "I hope whoever holds the winning numbers won't want a child and Ernest can be returned to us."

"Lizzie, I know you care deeply for the boy." Helen moistened her lips. "And in loving him, would you wish his return to an orphanage instead of being given a chance to grow up with a good family?"

"I—I know it sounds selfish," Lizzie whispered. "But it's not, entirely. I'm still praying for Nellie to return and claim him as her own." She turned to Jack. "We have a week. Could we search for her again?"

Jack's shoulders slumped. "Lizzie, it's been three weeks

since she left Ernest here."

"But she asked me to watch over him. If Nellie knew he might be taken away . . ."

"We've already hunted down every lead—every possibility."

"No—we haven't. We spent one afternoon!"

"I've returned to the railroad station several times a week since you and I went that first day." Jack rubbed his jaw. "I didn't tell you because I didn't want to get your hopes up. I found her apartment two days ago. It was tiny—and empty. Her neighbor said the landlord evicted her weeks ago because she couldn't pay rent, and that tenant didn't know where Nellie was going. There's nowhere else to look."

Eleven

How long had she been sitting under that maple tree? Lizzie swatted the fly that buzzed near her ear. Children's laughter filtered through the air. They played in the yard behind Brown Hall, oblivious to the horror taking place that day at the Alaska-Yukon-Pacific-Expo. An infant was being offered as a prize to strangers. All because the state superintendent for the Children's Home Society wanted to draw attention to the orphanage.

Not just any baby—the very one placed in her arms four weeks ago. The child who was given to her with a request from his mother to take care of her son and keep him safe. Ernest's welfare was no longer in Lizzie's control. Today, out of thousands of people entering the expo, someone would win precious Ernest. The little boy who had stolen Lizzie's heart.

She wrapped her arms around bent knees and buried her face in her arms. *Lord, I have no words . . .*

"Lizzie, are you all right?"

She peered up at Helen and shook her head. "No. I can't even pray."

"I can't *stop* praying. I sat in chapel this morning, but I didn't hear a word of the sermon." Helen perched her hands on her hips. "Did you have breakfast or lunch today?"

"I wasn't hungry."

"Lizzie, you've hardly eaten a bite all week. You need to keep up your strength."

"I appreciate your concern, but even the thought of food makes me nauseated." Lizzie's eyes watered. "I keep thinking about Ernest being presented for people to gawk at." She shuddered, despite the day's warmth. "My heart feels shriveled up and almost incapable of beating."

"I believe the superintendent had good intentions when he asked you to refrain from attending the expo today, but I'm glad Julia insisted on overseeing the child's care," Helen said. "Ernest is in good hands with her there, but I fear your heart would suffer even more if you were present."

Helen shook her head and sighed. "What a strange time we're living in. The exposition is also showcasing premature babies and charging admission to reimburse the costs of their care. The point of the exhibit is to draw attention to incubators, but I've heard many of the infants involved are orphans and not all are premature."

"I hope those babies are given proper care while on display." How long had Lizzie been immersed in her thoughts, attempting to escape from her pain? "What time is it?"

"The children will be expecting supper soon, and there is still work to be done." A ball bounced and landed a few feet from Helen. She threw the toy back to the young boy chasing after it. "But that's not why you're asking, is it?"

Lizzie could no longer control her tears, and several spilled from her lashes and trailed down her face. She shook her head. "No . . ."

"The drawing took place hours ago," Helen said quietly.

"So . . . it's done," Lizzie said, forcing the words past her lips. "Ernest may be leaving us soon."

"Remember, anyone adopting him must meet a list of qualifications. They won't hand over that sweet boy before making sure specific procedures are followed."

Jack arrived, driving the buggy instead of the wagon. He pulled up to the side of the building, jumped out, and tethered Shine.

Lizzie got to her feet and hurried toward him. "Jack!"

He waved, headed in her direction, and they met mid-point. "I couldn't wait to tell you." Was that relief on his face?

"Did you go to the expo?"

"I tried to stay home but couldn't—not today," he said, shaking his head.

"I've been sick with worry." Lizzie gestured toward the large maple. "Let's sit in the shade. I want to hear everything."

Without thinking about propriety, she grabbed his hand and pulled him forward, anxious to learn what would become of Ernest. But Jack didn't reject her touch. Instead, his warm, strong grip made her felt more secure in the uncertainty about the future.

They joined Helen, who hadn't left her post. "Jack, you have news?"

Lizzie reluctantly released his hand, almost embarrassed that Helen had witnessed her display, but he also seemed in no hurry to let go.

He wiped his brow, then as his gaze caught Lizzie's, his eyes filled with emotion, and she fought reaching out to him again. "Someone had the winning ticket, but no one came forward to claim Ernest."

"So . . . that means . . ." Lizzie held her breath, waiting to hear the joyous words.

"Whoever held the matching numbers either didn't want

to adopt a child or knew they wouldn't meet the requirements. Ernest is coming home to stay, at least for now."

Helen clapped her hands together. "Thank you, Jesus!"

Yes, thank you, Lord. "We have Ernest back in our care, and there's still a chance Nellie will return before he's adopted." Lizzie filled her lungs with fresh air. At the moment, she felt so light, she could imagine floating heavenward.

Jack's brow furrowed. "Lizzie . . ."

"I know—I know." Lizzie cocked her head. "I'm being unrealistic, and I need to keep my head out of the clouds. But one prayer has been answered. Why can't another be as well?"

☙

Julia had returned to Brown Hall with Ernest only minutes after Jack's report on the raffle's results. Lizzie ran to meet the carriage, and when the baby was placed in her arms, she clung to him and sobbed in relief. They'd come so close to losing this little boy.

After she fed him, Lizzie had put Ernest in the crib Timothy and his woodworking class had built for him. Although she'd have preferred to have kept the child close and held him all evening, Julia encouraged her to let him rest comfortably in bed. He'd had enough stimulation for one day.

Peace and quiet would help him slumber. Lizzie agreed, but that hadn't stopped her from checking on him often. She also needed to breathe, relax, and soak in the reality that the baby wouldn't be adopted by strangers only days later.

Her appetite returned, and Lizzie enjoyed the light supper of egg salad sandwiches, sliced tomatoes, and dill pickles. The night before, Helen and Emma had baked five chocolate cakes, just enough for each child and staff member to enjoy a taste. The desserts, frosted earlier that afternoon, were ready to serve that evening. The rare treat seemed fitting as they celebrated Ernest returning to Brown Hall for the foreseeable future.

Helen had also invited Jack to join them for the evening meal. Since his father didn't expect him to return in time for chores, he'd accepted. Jack even pitched in, making sandwiches. It was nice having him at the table, joking with Helen, sharing stories about his life on the farm.

Lizzie licked the taste of chocolate frosting clinging to her lips then sipped her coffee. Was she a horrible person? Should she be feeling so relieved that Ernest wasn't going to be adopted? It wasn't that she didn't want the little boy to have a family. She merely wanted to make sure that he was raised by someone who loved him, and Lizzie couldn't shake the feeling that Nellie was out there somewhere, still wanting to be his mother in every way possible.

Lizzie smiled as she observed Jack interact with Helen. His genuine concern for Ernest, as well as his kindness toward all made him even more attractive than his inviting smile and eyes that shared his soul. Lizzie felt warm and safe in his presence. If she were to develop feelings again for anyone, he would be a man like Jack. But still bearing the pain that came with losing Alex, how could she risk heartbreak again?

"Helen, you have visitors," Emma said, walking into the kitchen. "It's your nephew and his wife—Reverend and Mrs. Caswell. They're waiting in the front room."

"Oh, my goodness! I wasn't expecting them for another hour." Helen untied her apron and hung it on a hook. Her hands were quick to check her hair, and after pinning any loose strands back in place, she patted the sides of her head. "How do I look?"

"Lovely, as always," Lizzie said, giving her a quick squeeze.

"Thank you. We've exchanged so many letters over the years, I don't know why I'm suddenly nervous to meet them."

Emma smiled. "You don't have anything to worry about. They seem nice, and they're eager to see you." She spun back toward the hall entrance. "I offered to help in the nursery for a while. One of the babies is teething and causing a bit of a fuss."

"Would you please check on Ernest?" Lizzie asked.

"Of course. He's been on my mind too." Emma sauntered out of the kitchen with a grin on her face.

"I think what you're feeling may be more excitement than nerves, Helen." Lizzie took more plates from the cupboard. "We all want to meet them, so don't keep them waiting. There's a fresh pot of coffee brewed and plenty of cake to share."

Helen returned within minutes, beaming as bright as a harvest moon, and she brought with her a beautiful woman with eyes the color of blooming morning glories. The attractive man's hair matched his wife's dark shade, and his welcoming indigo blue eyes were striking. The couple likely turned heads wherever they ventured.

"Lizzie Clark—Jack Butler—please meet my nephew, Reverend Peter Caswell, and his wife, Mrs. Caswell." Helen gestured toward the table in the center of the kitchen where additional servings of dessert sat waiting for the newcomers. "Please—join us."

"Thanks, Auntie," the reverend said, holding out a chair for his wife. "And if you're willing, I'd like to go by my given name, Peter."

His wife smiled as she settled in at the table. "My husband and I are of like minds. Formalities aside, I'd prefer to be called Sarah. You're Helen's friends, and I hope you will become ours."

"I would like that very much." Lizzie poured Peter and Sarah a cup of coffee after they accepted her invitation.

They sat around the table as the Caswells relayed what they'd seen on their two-day train ride from Wisconsin to Seattle. They intended to explore the surrounding area and spend time with Helen, as well as spend several days at the expo.

Sarah's gram had died after being ill for months, but before she passed, she insisted that Sarah and Peter accomplish three things with the money she was leaving them. See the Pacific Ocean, meet Peter's aunt Helen in person, and go to the world's fair in Seattle. She wanted them to have a real vacation—a belated honeymoon.

"You have two children?" Lizzie asked.

"We do," Peter said as he accepted another pour of coffee from Helen. "Mary is eleven years old, and Joseph is five. They're staying with my sister's family on their farm."

"Ellie has three offspring of her own, and the cousins are quite fond of each other, so I imagine the children are having a grand time together." Sarah's eyes twinkled. "Fortunately, Ellie and her husband, Thomas, are adept at handling any mischief."

Helen reached over and placed her hand on top of her nephew's. "Of course I want to meet the entire family, but how nice that you were able to take this trip as a couple. A pastor's job must demand much of you at times."

"It does. But Sarah is a good listener, and her wisdom and support have saved me from myself. She reminds me that I can't fix people or relationships—only Jesus can. She's also far more patient than I am, so her perception is often helpful in challenging situations."

"Thank you." Sarah reached over and with a brief touch to her husband's face, demonstrated her affection.

What would it be like to have a marriage filled with so much love and devotion? Lizzie's heart grieved the loss of an intimate relationship she'd never experience with Alex or any other man.

"Pardon me?" Lizzie sensed she'd been asked a question while her thoughts were elsewhere.

"Peter and Sarah were asking if we could offer some guidance as to what they should see at the expo," Helen said.

"We assumed that everyone living in the area would have visited at some point these past months," Peter said. "But although Jack has spent time there, Helen mentioned that neither of you have been able to attend."

Sarah brightened. "Would it be possible for the five of us to go together? It would be so much fun to share the day with friends. Peter and I are taking the train to Moclips on Tuesday, and we're staying at a hotel on the beach for a couple of days, but we'll return to Seattle on Friday." She turned to Jack. "We plan to attend the expo on Saturday. Would you mind showing us the highlights?"

"I suppose I could join you, but I'm not much of a guide."

"It's not possible for both Lizzie and me to be absent from the kitchen," Helen chimed in, turning to Lizzie. "But if you'd like to go on Saturday, Emma and I can manage the meals. The older girls in training can help. And then, if you're willing to be in charge on Sunday, I'd like to spend that day with Peter and Sarah."

"Oh, I don't know . . ." Lizzie had taken an immediate liking to the Caswells, but could she enjoy herself, knowing that Ernest's future was still undetermined?

"I think you should have some fun, especially after this past week with all the worry about Ernest and the raffle's outcome," Helen said.

She thought she might go one day with Timothy, but Lizzie also didn't want to interfere if he wanted to enjoy the expo with Julia—alone. And with Peter and Sarah along, it wouldn't feel so much like a romantic outing with Jack as a group of friends spending the day together.

"Well, I have been eager to see the exhibits, so yes, I accept your generous invitation." It would be nice to put all concerns aside for a day. "I moved here earlier in August, and I didn't want to take time away from my work so soon after being employed. And then Ernest was placed in my care. My thoughts and time have been consumed with him since."

Sarah leaned forward, and her attention was completely focused on Lizzie. "Who is Ernest?"

She told them about Nellie and the baby, and Sarah's eyes teared as she listened to the tale of Ernest being left by his mother and then presented as a prize at the expo.

The veins in Peter's neck bulged. "It's horrifying that anyone—especially a man associated with an organization connected to faith—would consider giving a child away as a trophy!"

"In fairness, Nephew, there was no chance that the baby would have been given to anyone without assurance that the potential parents would provide a loving home for the boy."

Helen rubbed the rim of her cup with her thumb. "Still . . . we're thankful that he'll remain with us for now and is asleep in the nursery."

"From all that I've heard, God must have other plans for Ernest." Peter threw a glance at the individuals sitting around the table. "In due time, they'll be revealed."

Lizzie *wanted* to believe that—she *needed* to believe that. But if Nellie was a part of that plan, she couldn't wait too long to return.

Twelve

"What's wrong?" Lizzie's gaze flitted between Helen and Julia. They stood side by side in the kitchen, their heads cocked as they surveyed Lizzie. She checked her white shirtwaist for stains—nothing there.

Julia sighed and her eyebrows furrowed. "Your clothes."

"They're perfectly clean." Lizzie twisted left then right, checking for any flaws in her dark skirt.

"I think Julia is trying to point out that you often wear a similar wardrobe." Helen gave her a gentle smile. "This is a special day. You've put others first since you arrived at Brown Hall and have barely taken any time for yourself these past two months. You've waited so long to enjoy the expo, and now it's your turn to have some fun. Why not put on something pretty? My understanding is that visitors are showing up in their Sunday best."

"I don't know, Helen . . ." Lizzie had struggled with what to wear. She didn't want to give Jack the wrong impression—that she was trying to gain his attention. Though attracted to the kind man, she had no intention of getting involved in a romantic relationship, and he certainly hadn't indicated any interest in her outside of their mutual concern for Ernest.

Julia smiled. "This is the perfect occasion to show off that green day dress you brought with you."

Lizzie had been told numerous times that the garment's

shade—similar to lush green moss—was a lovely complement to her coloring. Perhaps she shouldn't be concerned by what Jack or anyone else might think. The apparel was comfortable, suitable for the slightly cool weather, and it made her feel feminine.

"All right. I have enough time to change. Jack, Peter, and Sarah are meeting me here." Lizzie made a dash for her room with excitement sparkling to the surface.

By the time she'd donned her dress and a black brimmed hat with a feather that matched her attire, Peter and Sarah were waiting in the kitchen with Helen. Sarah looked so pretty in her sky-blue dress with black and white trim, Lizzie was thankful she'd been encouraged to discard her simple dark skirt for the day.

She caught Jack's admiring smile as he entered the room moments later, and her face heated. His reaction caught her off guard. She shouldn't care that he approved of her appearance, but she also couldn't deny that it pleased her.

He'd surprised her by replacing his work shirt and pants with a dark suit and fashionable homburg hat. Lizzie tried not to stare, but he reminded her of the handsome heroes she'd read about in her copy of *Grimm's Fairy Tales*.

Jack hadn't seen Ernest for several days, so Julia brought him to the kitchen for them all to fawn over. Warmth flowed through Lizzie as Jack cradled the baby in his arms and allowed the child to hold his little finger. He remarked with pride how strong Ernest was getting, as if he himself were responsible for the infant's development.

The farmer's affection for the boy was evident in the way he carried Ernest and smiled down at him—until the infant started fussing. Then wide-eyed Jack sought Lizzie with a plea for help in his eyes. She grinned, ready to come to his aid, but Julia had warmed a bottle, and she took the hungry child back to the nursery to feed him.

As the foursome rode the trolley to the expo, Sarah and Peter shared how much they'd enjoyed staying at the Moclips Beach Hotel, built only twelve feet from the ocean shore. With more than three hundred rooms, it was the biggest hotel on the West Coast. The Caswells were grateful to have that special time together in such a beautiful location, and they'd spent their days inhaling the salty air, collecting shells for their children, and dreaming about their future.

Five minutes later, the trolley stopped at the entrance to the Alaska-Yukon-Pacific Exposition. Lizzie opened her purse and pulled out fifty cents for her admission fee.

Jack put his hand on hers. "Would you mind? I'd like to pay for you—my treat—as friends."

Lizzie didn't want to offend him, nor did she want to appear stubborn. She hesitated, then returned her coins to her purse. "Thank you, Jack. That's very generous, but I'll only accept your offer on one condition."

"And that is . . ."

"You allow me to later treat you to a lemonade—or anything else without alcohol." *Oh, dear.* Why did she say that? She shouldn't assume that he might want booze, and she didn't judge anyone who consumed spirits as long as they maintained control. But it would feel inappropriate for her provide such a drink.

Jack nodded and grinned. "You have a deal. And you have nothing to worry about. I'm not a drinker, and even if I were, liquor isn't allowed on the grounds."

"Oh, yes . . . I'd forgotten." Of course, she had. There was no reason for her to dwell on that rule.

Peter led them closer to the ticket booth. "I congratulate the officials. That decision couldn't have been easy."

"No one had a choice. There's a state law forbidding sale of liquor on any university campus. If they want a drink, people have to take a streetcar into downtown Seattle." Jack grinned. "I think the majority appreciate the absence of alcohol. Crime and general disturbances have been low, and some are giving credit to people not being influenced by booze."

They got their tickets and followed the crowd through three grand arches to the world's fair commemorating the Klondike Gold Rush.

Sarah stepped aside to allow a couple with four children to move on ahead. "My goodness, where do we begin?"

"Right here." Peter took his wife's hand and smiled down at her.

A short walk east revealed the George Washington statue with twelve thousand salmon-colored geraniums flanking each side and an array of gleaming structures that included the Fine Arts Building, the domed US Government Building, the Alaska Building, the smaller Washington Woman's Building, and the Agriculture Building.

The grounds were enhanced by colorful landscaping, sculptures, and waterfalls—a visual feast. Lizzie was mesmerized by the breathtaking atmosphere. Why had she waited so long to come?

They strolled down a path with a magnificent view of Mt. Rainier. If they continued, they'd eventually reach Lake Union, but for now, they focused on getting their bearings.

At the head of the spillway they discovered a round pool, the Arctic Circle, where a fountain called the Geyser spouted water ten stories into the sky. Jack explained it was modeled after Old Faithful at Yellowstone National Park, and it was supposed to be spectacular at night when illuminated by a thousand electric lights.

Jack stopped at the side of the path. "We could start with exploring some of the educational exhibits, or we could head in that direction to the midway. In keeping with the fair's Klondike theme, it's called the Pay Streak. There's a Ferris wheel, an amusement dubbed the Temple of Mirth, and a ride called the Haunted Swing."

Lizzie's curiosity was piqued, but would Peter and Sarah be more interested in venturing into more educational venues? If so, Lizzie would ask Timothy to return with her.

"The Pay Streak sounds exciting." Sarah gave her husband a charming smile. "And we'll never get another chance to experience something like this."

"We came for an adventure." Peter gave Jack a nod. "If everyone is agreeable to it, I say we head there."

Jack turned to Lizzie. "What do you think? If you'd rather not, I'll gladly stay with you, and we can do anything else you'd like."

"Oh, goodness, Jack." Lizzie scowled at him then laughed, relieved she wouldn't miss out on any potential fun. "Of course I want to go!"

They took in the view from the top of the Ferris wheel, and Sarah and Lizzie screamed with laughter while speeding along on the roller coaster. The Fairy Gorge Tickler, a ride where up to six people sat in a round bucket, twirled as it followed a curved, fenced-in trail down an incline.

Nervous and exhilarated, Lizzie's heart raced more from the possibility that she might bump or nudge up against Jack than from the ride itself. She unintentionally slammed into him twice and apologized, but he didn't seem to mind—not even a bit. Instead, he belly laughed almost as hard as Lizzie, but when she exited the bucket, she could barely catch her breath.

"The scent of roasting peanuts is making me hungry," Sarah said, covering her midsection with one hand.

"I smell popcorn." Lizzie relished the tempting aroma. "We could get something to nibble."

"Or we could fill our stomachs and eat again later." Jack winked at Lizzie.

"I agree with my friend." Peter pointed to the right. "There's a frankfurter stand over there, and it looks like they also serve root beer and sarsaparilla."

Sarah slipped her arm through Lizzie's. "I think the men might have a point. Are you willing?"

Lizzie chuckled. "Does admitting that I'm actually famished answer your question?"

The two women led the way to the stand, and after ordering, Lizzie retrieved money from her purse to pay for her food as well as Jack's. When he protested, she planted her feet in front of him and raised an eyebrow. "Jack, we agreed that if you paid for my entry into the expo, you would allow me to treat you to something inside. Are you refusing to follow through on our deal?"

"All right, I'll concede. And thank you." Jack grabbed a root beer for himself and a sarsaparilla for Lizzie from the gentleman overseeing the food stand. They stepped back to allow Sarah and Peter to order. "I'm curious. Why were you stubborn about paying? Most women like it when a man takes care of things."

"Perhaps I'm not like most women." Should she try to explain? Lizzie took a deep breath. "You and I talked about the suffrage movement and women being given more rights. But my choices go beyond that. As a woman, I feel like I have to always prove that I can take care of myself. I don't need a man to survive. I'm capable of accomplishing that on my own."

"I understand the desire to demonstrate skills and strengths and be appreciated for them." Jack took a drink then caught Lizzie's gaze with his. "But I don't think it's necessary or even possible to go through life without any help. Everyone needs a hand now and then, and they shouldn't be afraid or ashamed to ask for it," he said thoughtfully.

"It's not that I don't see the value in giving and receiving assistance. We all have different God-given gifts that can and should be used to help others. But there are reasons why it's important for me to feel self-sufficient."

Sarah joined them with her hands full, but she nodded to her right. "There's a small table over there with room for all four of us. Peter went to claim it."

Relieved at the interruption, Lizzie followed her without asking Jack if he had anything else to say about her independence. Men had more choices. People didn't question their desire or determination to make something of themselves outside of marrying and creating a family. Was it possible for Jack to understand her position?

Musicians seated in a nearby bandstand struck up the tune, "Meet Me in Seattle, Dearie, in 1909," and that was followed by the fair's official march, "Gloria Washington."

"It's wonderful to hear music throughout the grounds," Sarah said, sounding content.

"It is nice." Peter leaned over and gave his wife's hand a

brief squeeze. "We have talented musicians in Riverton, but it's a small town. Our exposure to different forms is limited."

"You'll have opportunities to see a variety of performances while visiting the expo. Entertainers have come from all over the United States *and* the world." Jack drummed his fingers on the table in beat with the current tune being played.

Lizzie laughed. "I think I've read everything the *Seattle Times* has printed on the expo, and Jack is right. If you want to see and hear something different, participating countries are sharing their musical traditions."

"Oh, my." Sarah's shoulder sagged, and she gave a slight frown. "It feels like we could spend every day for a week at the fair and still not experience everything."

"Don't worry, Sarah." Peter chuckled. "We'll see plenty, and before you know it, you'll be eager to get home and hug our children."

"You're right, dear husband. I should savor every minute here while I can and not concern myself about anything else."

Lizzie had known the couple for only a week, but they already felt like close friends. She was going to miss them when they left. "If music is a priority, big-time bands from Chicago and New York, a Southern vaudeville revue, and popular headliners from Seattle are all here. The Seattle Symphony is also providing a regular Sunday afternoon concert series at the Auditorium, so if you or Helen are interested, you'll be able to attend one of their performances tomorrow."

They finished eating and continued exploring. The Pay Streak was often the busiest, loudest, most crowded portion of the exposition grounds with its entertainment, games, and exhibits. The Baby Incubator Exhibit, housed in a two-story neoclassical pavilion featuring Ionic columns and graced by ornamental pilasters and window moldings, was built between the Temple of Palmistry and the Gold Camps of Alaska.

"Do you want to go in?" Jack asked. "Or will it be too disturbing?"

How kind of him to be sensitive to her feelings about Ernest having been on display prior to the raffle drawing. "I'm not sure—"

"It would be entirely understandable if you wanted to avoid the place," Sarah said with empathy. "We can move on."

"Thank you—to all of you—for being so considerate." Lizzie took a deep breath, grateful for such caring friends. "But I think it might be helpful to see the exhibit, and we came here to not only be entertained but to also be educated. If this is part of our country's future and how children will be cared for, perhaps it's important that we learn more."

Admission was charged to reimburse the costs of the babies' care, and fairgoers filed into the viewing room. A rail separated patrons from the incubators, which were enclosed, heated, and ventilated glass boxes. The babies rested inside, wrapped in blankets.

Female attendants wearing nurse uniforms and a male attendant in a white lab coat stood by. High transom windows admitted light and air, and the ceiling was stenciled with an ivy design. Live potted palms were placed between the incubators, and weight-bearing support columns were designed to resemble palm trees. Visitors were informed that periodic lectures would be given on incubator technology and other aspects of scientific infant care.

The infants seemed well taken care of, although not all seemed small enough to be premature. Lizzie's heart went out to each one. "I wonder if all the babies exhibited are really orphans, even though the *Seattle Times* has reported that some of them have been adopted during the course of the fair."

Jack scratched his head. "There's a daycare center attached to the exhibit so fairgoers can leave their children to be watched by the exhibition's nurses, so perhaps not all are without families."

Before they left the Pay Streak, they encountered the Igorrote Village, populated by natives from the Philippine island of Luzon. Reputed to be headhunters and dog-eaters, the Igorrotes laughingly engaged in dances, spear-throwing contests, and cloth weaving.

Lizzie's face flushed with heat at seeing the men wearing only loincloths. Should she turn away? "Isn't this wrong—to have those people on display and almost naked? And for people to laugh about their way of life?"

"I understand why you'd feel that way. People can be cruel in these situations," Peter said in a kind and patient tone. "Missionaries to other countries are often faced with the same dilemma—how to deal with traditions and ways of life that are unfamiliar or don't feel right by our standards."

"When the loincloths worn by men and boys became a moral issue early on during the expo, a reverend and a respected judge were assigned to investigate." Jack gave Lizzie an understanding smile. "They determined the loincloths were native dress and not intended to titillate. And it may not make much difference to some of us, but the Igorrotes are being compensated for their performances."

"Perhaps inviting them here is one way to not only educate them but also us," Sarah said, sounding wise.

Lizzie nodded. It helped to gain more information and

hear her friends' perspectives, but she still couldn't shake the feeling that the Igorrotes were being mistreated.

The four made a pact to set aside all seriousness for the rest of the day.

Although only two foreign nations, Canada and Japan, had erected major buildings, an international flavor was created by a Chinese village, Eskimo villages, a Bohemian restaurant, a Vienna café, the Spanish Theatre, a Formosa Tea Room, Italian gondola rides, and a Streets of Cairo exhibit featuring a camel and a belly dancer.

The California Building was designed in the style of a Spanish mission. It contained a life-size elephant created out of walnuts, an almond cow, and a bear made from raisins. Hawaii showcased a thirty-foot-high pyramid of coconuts and pineapples. The forestry building was built out of wood and actual tree trunks. Alaska's exhibit awed them with a heavily guarded display of gold dust, nuggets, and bricks said to be worth a million dollars. The case descended into an underground vault at night.

The Streets of Cairo and the Klondyke Dance Hall were venues where attendees could watch risqué exhibitions. These two places were known to be frequently shut down by the morality enforcers at the expo. Lizzie had no interest in getting close to either building, and she was pleased that Jack showed no curiosity either.

The first airplanes were on exhibit. The Wright brothers had only flown a few years before. Bud Meyers was hired to fly his dirigible around the fairgrounds. Because the contraption had no seat, he had to straddle a metal device.

Dazzling buildings, various art forms, cutting-edge technology, and music from around the world. It was all a visual and educational feast for visitors. It was the closest most people would ever get to traveling to Rome, New York, Athens, or Paris. For Lizzie and her friends—an experience of a lifetime.

Exhilarated by the sights, sounds, and tastes of the exposition, each of the four also acknowledged that they were physically exhausted from walking all day, so they headed toward the entrance. The fair would remain open until midnight, and as the sun set, the grounds lit up, illuminated by hundreds of thousands of electrical lights.

"Oh, how enchanting!" Lizzie spun around slowly, taking in another example of what the future could possibly hold. "I've never seen anything so extraordinary."

"Scientists and inventors are changing the world." Peter grinned. "Automobiles that can make it across the entire country, machines that can carry men through the air, electricity that can light up the sky for miles—and incubators that can provide a temporary womb for a tiny baby."

"I can't imagine what will come next," Sarah said.

A mischievous smile crossed Jack's face. "Perhaps one day, people will even travel to the moon."

Peter burst out with a loud laugh. "Sure, Jack—sure."

As they approached the gate, Lizzie stopped, alarmed by a loud disturbance on the other side of the entrance. "Do you hear that?"

Jack nodded. "Sounds serious."

Sarah grasped Peter's hand, and they followed Jack and Lizzie.

A crowd had gathered outside, and the air was filled with loud chatter as onlookers questioned each other, all trying to get answers as to the cause of the commotion.

"I'll see what I can find out." Jack pushed his way through

the mass and disappeared for a few minutes. He returned somber. "Earlier today, a streetcar jumped the tracks and hit three concession buildings. Fifty-five people were injured—men, women, and children. A man from Tacoma died."

"Is there anything we can do to help?" Peter asked.

Jack shook his head. "Ambulances have already taken the seriously wounded, and other medical personnel are here taking care of the others. Police are also on-site. I think the best thing we can do is leave the area."

"How tragic." Sarah slipped her arm through her husband's and nestled close to him. "It's moments like these that remind me not to take anything for granted. We need to appreciate each day and not waste opportunities."

Lizzie walked with her friends back to Brown Hall. They fell into silence, possibly, like her, needing time to think about what they'd just witnessed and the fragility of life.

The dim streetlights—so different from the brilliance of those at the fair—still provided enough radiance to find their way. Before long, they entered the orphanage's welcoming kitchen where Helen sat at the table, her head propped up by her right hand.

She stood, and her face filled with concern. "Oh, dear . . . I can't imagine how you've heard already."

"Helen, what are you talking about?" Lizzie placed her hand on the woman's shoulder.

"I thought—you all look so forlorn—I assumed." Helen's fingertips briefly touched her lips. "Didn't you have a nice time at the fair?"

Sarah laid her purse on the table. "The exposition was wonderful! We had a delightful day. Something else has us a bit downhearted."

"There was an accident involving a streetcar, and a lot of people were injured." Jack checked the coffeepot sitting on the stove then pulled cups from the cupboard. "One man died."

Helen dropped into her chair. "I'm so sorry to hear that. How horrible for those people—that man's family."

"But there's something else, isn't there?" Lizzie sat next to Helen, then she accepted a cup of hot coffee from Peter and nodded her thanks.

The moisture filling Helen's eyes reflected the glow from a nearby lamp. "I have some news, and I don't know how you'll take it."

Thirteen

"Helen, what's wrong?" All the joy captured throughout the day escaped Lizzie, and she braced herself. "Did something happen to my brother? To Ernest?"

"No," Helen said, moving out of her slump and sitting straight. "No one has been harmed. But a couple met Reverend Brown here this afternoon because they want to adopt a baby boy. Julia told me that Ernest is one of two infants they're considering."

That announcement sucked all the air from Lizzie's lungs. She couldn't speak, and a glance at Jack's expression revealed he possibly also felt punched in the stomach.

"I'm confused." Peter sat next to Sarah at the table. "Isn't that a positive thing? For a child to be placed in a home with people who want to be parents?"

"In most cases, yes." Helen wrung her hands. "But when the reverend left the office for a short time to tend to another matter, the door was left partly open. Julia and I overheard the visitor be harsh with his wife, and he said some things."

"And they made you concerned," Lizzie said softly.

Helen sighed and nodded. "Julia and I are worried that if they choose one of our boys, he'll be adopted for the sole purpose of being used as a laborer on the farm. The gentleman—if I can even call him that—wants an older boy to help with chores, but the woman has somehow convinced him that a baby could be raised to obey and not rebel. They'd have a clean slate as opposed to dealing with a child who has already formed some attachments and opinions."

Sarah grasped her husband's hand. "That woman sounds manipulative and almost as bad as her husband."

"I'm not so sure." Helen rubbed her eyes. "I observed her when I got a chance, and I think she has a gentle nature. She may even be nurturing."

"But if she's willing to bring an infant into a home where the potential father may be a brute?" Lizzie frowned and shook her head. "How can that be in the best interest of the child?"

"Not intentionally being a bit conniving, the woman may simply be hungry for someone to love and for someone to actually love her," Sarah said with compassion.

"Possibly." Helen lifted her cup, then she hesitated and set it back on the table. "Most people might think it's better to place a child in a home than in an orphanage, but in some cases, I don't believe that's true. Here at Brown Hall, we defend and love them like our own—at least, we try to look out for them."

Prior to coming to the orphanage, Lizzie had never considered that an adoption might put a child in harm's way, but now that Ernest's future was at stake, she was completely invested in wanting the best for him. "Helen, is there anything we can do?"

"Julia and I talked to Reverend Brown about what we overheard. A second interview is taking place tomorrow, but the couple will most likely be declined." Helen's gaze traveled between Lizzie and Jack. "However, what happened today does raise the possibility that Ernest will be adopted by someone, and you'll need to let him go, whether you like the people or not."

"I'm not sure I can accept that." Lizzie almost choked on her words. Both Helen and Timothy had warned her about the dangers of getting overly attached, but how could she not? "Nellie put me in charge of taking care of Ernest. I don't know if that means keeping him safe until she can return or making sure he gets a good home. She wasn't entirely clear in the letter she left behind."

With her thoughts racing, Lizzie stood and paced. "And what if—despite the Children's Home Society trying to ensure every child will be placed in a good home—what if even with the best intentions, something gets missed? And what if Ernest doesn't get adopted?"

What if Lizzie, in her role as cook at the orphanage, couldn't offer him what he needed to grow and thrive? Everyone at Brown Hall tried to give the children excellent care, but the staff was stretched. "What if Nellie comes back for Ernest? And he's not here?" Lizzie would have failed her friend, and a mother and son would be separated with no hope of being reunited.

Jack had stood silent through their conversation, but now he placed his hands on Lizzie's shoulders and stopped her in the middle of the kitchen. "I have a solution."

Everyone turned their focus on the pair.

"Marry me, Lizzie. Marry me, and we'll adopt Ernest and provide a home for him together."

☙

Did he just blurt that out? A marriage proposal? Jack hadn't given it much thought—not any, really—but it made sense, didn't it?

Lizzie froze in place, gawking at Jack like he was crazy. "You want to get married? Just like that?"

He'd surprised her and shocked himself. "Maybe we should talk about this outside—alone." Jack gave a side glance to the three people sitting at the kitchen table, and he glimpsed Helen's pleased smile.

"I—I suppose we should." Without giving anyone more acknowledgment, Lizzie grabbed her shawl hanging on a hook nearby. She wrapped it around her shoulders, then headed outside.

"Jack, we'll be praying for you both," Peter said.

"Thanks." Jack closed the door behind him and followed Lizzie to the largest maple tree in the backyard. They sat on the bench placed beneath its canopy.

The breeze rustled the leaves, and Lizzie drew the wrap tighter around her. Soft beams of light emanated from the kitchen windows, allowing Jack to view her furrowed brows and the way she chewed the corner of her lip.

"Is it getting too cold to sit out here?" It wouldn't help if she was chilled. Their conversation was enough to make them feel uncomfortable.

"No, I'm fine," she whispered.

Her tone didn't sound angry or frustrated—only thoughtful. "Are you considering my offer?"

"Offer?" Now Lizzie sounded irritated. "That sounds more like a business proposition than a proposal. What are we doing here, Jack?"

"I'm sorry. That came out wrong." She was right. He shouldn't have approached marriage that way. "And I shouldn't have asked in front of our friends, but in the moment, it seemed like a logical answer to the situation."

"Logical?" She wasn't making this easy.

Maybe he'd made a huge mistake in thinking getting married would solve one problem when it might only create a heap more.

"I'm not great with words." He filled his lungs and leaned back against the bench. How could he explain? "I just thought . . . we both feel responsible for making sure Ernest has a good home. He might be adopted and taken away from us. If that happens, we'll never see him again and know for sure that he's safe and happy. And it would also mean there would be no chance of Nellie seeing her son again. Am I wrong?"

Lizzie shook her head. "No."

"Would you consider adopting Ernest alone?" As soon as the words slipped out, he regretted saying them. A feeling of potential loss shadowed his heart. It wouldn't feel right—him not being a part of their lives.

"It might not be possible. The orphanage will want to find a couple willing to provide a home—a family—for Ernest."

"That's what I figured." Jack shifted and moved a tad closer to Lizzie. He enveloped her cool, feminine hand in his and was relieved when she didn't pull away. Why was it so hard to admit that he enjoyed her touch? "I have a small house on the farm, big enough for the three of us."

"I won't make promises I can't keep," she said with sadness. "I can't give my heart to another man—I just can't."

"I understand. I'm not asking you to." Jack felt the same way. He wasn't willing to expose his heart and risk getting hurt either. Loss had destroyed them both in the past. Lizzie's fiancé, the love of her life, had died before they could begin a life together. And as a young boy, Jack had experienced his mother's rejection. "That's why it could be perfect. It wouldn't be a conventional marriage. You could have your own bedroom with the baby."

"But where would you sleep?"

"I'd bunk in my father's house until I could build on two additional bedrooms to my—our—place."

"A marriage of convenience? Based on friendship alone?"

"Yes. Not a business arrangement, but we'd have a partnership of sorts." Visions of how life *could be* formulated in Jack's mind. "We're both independent people, right? We like each other and seem to get along. But you're still in love with Alex, and I have no interest in getting romantically involved with anyone."

His mother's leaving made it difficult for him to trust women, with Helen and Lizzie being the exceptions. Even if he was drawn to Lizzie, how could he ever reveal his feelings, knowing that her heart still belonged to someone else?

Jack cleared his throat. He had to say it and make it clear. "You don't need to worry about any expectations on my part for having marital relations. I won't place either of us in that situation."

Lizzie sniffed and pulled a handkerchief from her skirt pocket. Then she adjusted her shawl and turned away. With her back toward him, he could only imagine that she was dabbing her nose or wiping her tears. Reactions caused by the chilled air? Or something else?

Now *he* felt uncomfortable. It wasn't that he lacked desire. He was human, after all, but he would never obligate even a wife to share his bed. What was intimacy without trust? If she couldn't give herself completely to him without any reservations because her loyalty remained elsewhere, Jack couldn't risk being vulnerable.

Lizzie shifted and faced him, still gripping the handkerchief in one hand. "Due to the nature of your proposal—your request to create a *partnership*—my decision will be based merely on what I think might be best for Ernest."

"I understand." So, he was right. His heart clenched with physical pain. Any interest Lizzie had shown was purely about protecting the baby.

She sat quiet for a moment, then she released a heavy sigh. "What about my job here at the orphanage?"

"You're free to do as you please. It's unlike a teacher's position where you would have to give it up if married. If you want to continue cooking here, we'll figure something out for Ernest while you're working."

"Are you sure you want to do this, Jack?" Lizzie sounded unconvinced. "You confessed once that you would never marry after what your mother did to your family."

"I'm not searching for anything unrealistic—a fantasy. I'm merely committing to raising Ernest together."

"What if Nellie comes back? What would that mean for us? For our marriage?" Lizzie placed her hand on his arm as though to make sure he was paying attention. "And . . . there's something else we need to talk about."

"Your own café."

"I can't let that dream slip away, Jack."

Fourteen

J ack stepped out onto the back porch and claimed the empty rocker. Stars surrounded the quarter moon in the dark sky. Gray wisps carrying the sweet scent of vanilla mixed with cherries rose from his father's lit pipe. LeRoy Butler rarely smoked—and only when he had much to mull over.

"You're home awfully late." Jack's father moved his rocker in a steady, slow rhythm. "You have a nice time at the expo?"

"I did. The Caswells are good people."

"I'm glad you enjoyed yourself. About time you had some fun." His father halted and faced Jack, the dim light from the sky revealing nothing about his expression. "And Miss Clark? Is she good people too?" His gentle tone relayed sincere interest.

"Yes. Lizzie is quite extraordinary." Jack couldn't keep his proposal a secret, but how could he possibly explain what might sound like a rash decision? "I—I asked her to marry me."

"Jack . . ." Was that disappointment in his father's voice?

"She hasn't given me her answer yet. I'm going back to the orphanage on Monday night after we've both had more time to think about our decisions." Jack leaned forward and scrubbed his face with his hands. "I know we haven't known each other for long, but Lizzie is smart and compassionate. And we want to adopt Ernest."

"So, this is all about Nellie's son?"

"He needs a loving family with parents who will look out for his best interests—not take him into their home to provide free labor."

"Surely there are decent people who adopt children. They can't all be monsters."

"No, of course they're not."

"Look, Jack . . . you're a man who places loyalty above almost anything else. I remember what Nellie did for you and how her sacrifice made you feel. And though it may not often seem like it, I haven't forgotten what you gave up, staying on the farm to help me and your brother."

"I do owe Nellie, but that isn't the entire story."

"Still, I question the rationale behind your decision to propose." His father raised the pipe to his mouth then lowered it without taking a puff. "Do you have feelings for Lizzie?"

"I like her."

"But you don't love her."

"We barely know each other—remember?" So how was Jack to know for sure what he felt for Lizzie? He could be fooling himself, and besides, she was only interested in keeping Ernest safe.

"It doesn't always take a long time to know how you feel about another person. I fell for your mother the day I met her."

"And look how that turned out," Jack said, his voice filled with bitterness. "If you're using your experience to dissuade me, you don't have to worry. I'll never trust a woman with my heart—not after what my mother did to yours. And don't forget . . . she not only left you, she walked away from me and Adam too."

"I would never discourage you from marrying the right woman, Jack. I'm actually happy that you're willing to think about taking a wife someday." His father sighed. "If you have true feelings for Lizzie, that's one thing. But it's not fair to either of you if this union is only about paying a debt. I don't want you to risk losing your chance at true love—the kind that runs deep."

"I'm not sure I can believe that exists."

"Jack, you watched me struggle after your mother left, and though I'm a bit scarred, I'm still standing. One hurtful experience doesn't mean all women will let you down."

"Maybe."

"And maybe if I'd been open to another relationship instead of closing myself off, I'd have someone special to care for now myself. Sure, I love you and your brother, but I miss having a companion to talk to late at night about our day—our future."

"I didn't know . . ."

"If you marry Lizzie, I hope you'll accept the possibility of love growing between the two of you. Don't blame her and every other woman for your mother's choices. They were hers and hers alone."

Fifteen

L izzie might not have been missed at chapel if she hadn't attended that morning, but moments in prayer had been far more valuable than the additional hour in the kitchen she would have gained. Her quiet reflection was followed by a flurry of activity as Emma and two other girls assisted Lizzie in making lunch for those living at Brown Hall.

With so much on her mind, she hadn't slept the night before. Her thoughts had been kidnapped by Jack's proposal. If she could call it that. It was more of a proposition—a way to ensure that Ernest would have loving parents. Lizzie yawned and rubbed her eyes.

Not much left to do in the kitchen for now. If her aides took care of those remaining tasks, she could slip away to her room and rest before starting supper—simple sandwiches, cucumber salad, and apple slices.

Helen had offered to return that afternoon to help with last-minute preparations for the evening meal, but Lizzie had encouraged her to stay as long as she wanted at the expo. Time spent with Peter and Sarah was precious, and Helen deserved a day away from the kitchen to enjoy herself.

"Harriet and Kathryn." Lizzie waited for their full attention. "Would you please finish cleaning the pots and pans? There are only a few to wash."

"Yes, Miss Clark," Kathryn said.

"I appreciate your help, girls." Lizzie stifled a second yawn. "Emma, would you mind tidying up the rest of the kitchen? You know how Helen likes everything in place."

Emma grinned. "I sure do!"

"Thanks, Em." Lizzie stepped outside and inhaled the brisk air. Children, scattered across the yard, were releasing pent-up energy before they'd be called in and required to read in silence for an hour.

The bench beneath the tree beckoned her, and she maneuvered around a group playing tag, avoiding collision with anyone. She slid onto the seat, not even minding the hard surface. Her heavy eyelids closed, but their reprieve didn't last long. Lizzie sensed another body next to hers, and she opened her eyes. "Timothy."

"You mentioned at lunch that you wanted to talk privately." Her brother's eyes narrowed, and he studied her. "What's going on, Lizzie? You look—"

She gave him a weak smile. "Exhausted? Distracted? Worried?"

"All those things and more." His forehead furrowed. "Should I be concerned?"

"No—yes—possibly." Lizzie sighed then forced herself to look at him. "Jack asked me to marry him."

Her brother's eyebrows shot up, and his mouth gaped. "He proposed?"

"In front of Helen, Peter, and Sarah."

"You've only known each other for what—a month?"

"Five weeks," Lizzie said quietly.

"Oh, forgive me," he said, raising his hands. "*That* makes a difference."

"Don't you want to know what I said?" She didn't mean to sound defensive, but he wasn't giving her a chance to explain.

"I'm assuming you politely declined."

"I haven't given him an answer yet," she said, trying to control her rising frustration. "He's coming back tomorrow night after supper. Just to talk. He's not pressuring me to decide."

"Lizzie, I like Jack. I do. But you can't seriously be considering marriage."

"Why not?" Her eyes burned from the hot liquid pooling in them, and her face warmed. Timothy wasn't making this any easier for her. If *he* was doubting her judgment, maybe getting married was a mistake.

"Because you're not ready. You're still in love with Alex."

"I'll *always* love Alex."

"Yes, I believe you will. But in time, your heart will heal, and you'll have a better chance of sharing similar feelings with another man. Why would you marry someone you don't love—and barely even know?"

"Ernest."

Timothy stared at her for a moment, then his shoulders slumped. "This is about the baby."

"Jack and I care deeply for Nellie's child, and we both feel responsible for him." Lizzie grasped her brother's hand. "I can't stand the thought of that little boy being placed in a home where he might not be the sun, the moon, and the stars to his new parents. As a couple, Jack and I would be able to adopt and raise him."

"Lizzie, you're focusing only on the infant's future. What about your own? You've been so determined to be in control of your life. What if you lose any further opportunity? And why would you be willing to throw away the possibility of finding someone to share a love-filled marriage?"

"Timothy . . ."

"And I don't understand why you feel such loyalty to a woman you met only weeks before the child's birth."

She freed her brother's hand. "You've forgotten that Nellie asked *me*—not the orphanage—to take care of her son," Lizzie said with an edge to her tone. She'd never had to defend her feelings or her actions to him before. Why was he being so disagreeable now?

"I know it may not make sense, but I felt closer to Nellie in that short time than I'd ever felt with any other friends—aside from you, that is." Lizzie calmed her voice again. "I don't want to argue. I value your opinions, and I wanted to talk through my decision."

"I'm sorry." He put his arm around her shoulder and drew her close. "I should be listening and helping you figure out what you want to do. Instead, I've sounded like I was accusing you of being incapable of an intelligent evaluation of the situation."

Lizzie tittered. "Evaluation of the situation?" She lifted her gaze. His lips quirked mischievously. The endearing brother she counted on had returned.

"Tell me more about this *proposal* of Jack's and why you're giving it serious thought."

"He's a kind, hardworking man who truly cares about Ernest. I believe with my entire being that Jack would be a wonderful father." Lizzie smiled as his qualities came to mind. "And he's extremely loyal. I know that to be true. The reason he first became invested in the baby's welfare is because of his and Nellie's childhood friendship. That much you've known, but he also put his own aspirations aside to help his father and give his brother the opportunity to become a veterinarian."

"Seems pretty unselfish."

"It is, and he continually shows generosity to the orphanage."

"But what about the two of you?"

"There's mutual respect, and we genuinely like each other."

"That's a start."

"It wouldn't be like an arranged marriage. We'd be making our own decision to commit to each other." Lizzie folded her arms across her chest. There was something else she needed to be honest about—with herself and her brother. "What if I never get over Alex? What if, deep down, I don't want to? At least with Jack, I'd have some companionship—friendship. More than what I'd have on my own as a spinster." She looked into her brother's adoring eyes. "And isn't friendship important in a marriage?"

He nodded. "You've done more evaluating than what I expected."

"I have." She smiled. "And I hope that you'll be proud of me for also not forgetting about my own dreams."

"The restaurant? You talked about that—with him?" Timothy asked with a tone that relayed both surprise and pride.

"I couldn't consider marrying Jack without making it clear that running my own restaurant is non-negotiable. I will find an avenue to start my own business."

"Good for you, Lizzie."

"In the meantime, he promised to not stand in the way of my work at the orphanage. I asked Helen what would happen to my job if I married and had a baby of my own. She said I could bring an infant with me for a few months, but before long, I'd need to find someone to care for the child. We couldn't have a crawler or a toddler underfoot while cooking, and the staff is already too busy with caring for the orphans living here."

"That makes sense."

"But if I were my own boss, I would also need help with a child. That would have been the case if Alex and I'd married and had a family of our own. The good news—Jack is supportive of my restaurant dreams."

"Dear Sister, it sounds like you've made up your mind."

Have I?

Lizzie nestled into her brother. What she hadn't mentioned was her physical and emotional attraction to Jack—a secret she'd keep to herself. Jack had confessed that he wasn't interested in turning his heart over to any woman. Not after what his mother did to his family. Lizzie couldn't take the risk of being broken again. She might not have the strength to put all the pieces back together if that happened.

Sixteen

L izzie had requested sole use of Brown Hall's library for an hour that evening so she and Jack could talk freely without being interrupted. The kitchen was continuously invaded, and it would be inappropriate for the two of them to spend time alone in her room.

Flames crackling in the fireplace cast a warm glow on Jack as he held Ernest in the chair next to hers. The child lay sleeping comfortably in his arms, and the soon-to-be father seemed quite relaxed, considering the serious responsibility he was about to undertake.

If she accepted Jack's proposal, would Lizzie often experience this strange sense of contentment? She'd spoken with Timothy and shared her concerns about marriage but also the excitement she felt within. Life with Jack could be good, and since they'd come to an understanding about her aspirations, she wouldn't be hindered like she might be as a single woman.

Even more important—Ernest would be loved and protected.

After Alex's death, Lizzie had prepared herself to never find love again, and it wouldn't be fair to expect Jack to treat their commitment to each other like anything other than a partnership. But sitting here with him, with tender feelings stirring inside whenever he glanced her way and smiled, as though they shared a secret, questions needled her thoughts.

Her feelings for Jack had already grown over the past weeks, and they might intensify as they spent more time together. Could she remain satisfied with their arrangement? Or was she venturing into territory that would produce hurtful rejection? It felt imperative to guard herself.

Jack's gaze moved from the little boy to her. "He's asleep."

"Ernest feels secure with you." Lizzie's heart fluttered as Jack's intelligent brown eyes held hers.

"I hope he'll always feel that way." He stroked the child's cheek gently. "And you? Have you come to a decision? Can you trust me enough to take my name?"

"When Nellie left Ernest in my care, she wanted me to keep him safe. She didn't ask me to find him a home."

"True . . . if you don't leave any room for interpretation."

"What if Nellie returns for Ernest? What do we do then? Will we have wed for nothing?"

Jack focused on the infant and sighed. "Nellie's not coming back. If she had any intention of doing so, she would have made that clear. And I don't believe that you and I becoming parents to Ernest would be a mistake."

She agreed, but she'd also wanted that assurance from him. Still, this important decision couldn't be based on feelings alone. *Lord, I've prayed many times about my answer, and I need confirmation now. Please. What am I supposed to do?*

Peace washed over Lizzie like a delicate spring shower, and she inhaled a light, sweet fragrance. *Thank you, Lord.* "Yes. My answer is yes."

His head jerked back to her. "Yes?"

She nodded and smiled.

Jack grinned in return, and his countenance lit up like a child's who had won the biggest prize at the fair. "I'll do my best to never disappoint you."

"I know you will, and I promise to do my part as well. I want our little family to be happy. All three of us."

He reached his hand toward her, and she grasped it, feeling his warmth and strength. It wasn't a kiss, but the gesture still felt intimate. "How do you feel about having the wedding soon?"

"I think it's best." She slipped her hand from his, then regretted severing that physical connection. "Reverend Brown could perform the ceremony, but what would you think about asking Peter? We haven't known them long, but he and Sarah already feel like family."

"I like that idea, but they leave Seattle on Saturday."

"It wouldn't give us much time to prepare, but we could arrange something small and private for Friday evening." Details flooded Lizzie's thoughts. "I'd like my parents to be here, as well as Timothy and Julia, Helen, Emma, and my brother, Joseph." She turned to Jack. "That's my family and two friends, but you must have people you'd like present."

"My dad." He thought for a moment. "My brother, Adam, and his wife are expecting their own child any day. It might not be possible for them to come, but I'll invite them, regardless."

Lizzie stood. "We should talk to Peter."

"Now?"

"We don't have time to dawdle." She reached for the five-week-old baby and cradled him against her chest. "We can leave Ernest in the nursery. He won't wake for another feeding for two to three hours."

"I don't want to dampen your enthusiasm, but is it poor manners to show up at Helen's without an invitation?"

"You're considerate to point that out." Lizzie kissed the baby's forehead softly. "Helen is expecting us."

Jack's forehead furrowed. "I don't understand." He stood and rubbed the back of his neck. "How long ago did you decide to marry me?"

"Tonight—right before I said yes." Lizzie smiled. "I didn't keep you in suspense for fun. I told Helen that you were coming to visit Ernest, and she invited us to join them for dessert. I didn't commit, but she insisted that we'd be welcome, regardless."

"You're a wonder, Lizzie Clark." He gave her a broad grin. "I can only hope and pray that I'm smart enough to keep up with you."

Twenty minutes later, Ernest was tucked in his crib, and Lizzie and Jack were seated at Helen's dining room table with her, Sarah, and Peter.

Lizzie pushed a bite of spice cake around the plate with her fork. Helen's layered masterpiece looked delicious, but Lizzie had suddenly lost her appetite. What if their friends thought the decision to marry and adopt Ernest was foolish?

"What's going on, Lizzie?" Helen asked as she refilled Peter's coffee cup. "You and Jack seem out of sorts tonight."

"Time to be up-front as to why we're here," Jack said, keeping his eyes on Lizzie. "We came to talk about Ernest and how he deserves to have a real family with two parents."

Peter glanced at Sarah, and she returned his disturbed expression. He laid his forearms on the table and leaned forward. "Did you come to ask us to adopt Ernest?"

Jack paled—or was that Lizzie's imagination?

"No—that's not why we've come." Lizzie wet her lips. "You and Sarah would be wonderful parents, and I know that Ernest would be happy with you. But we never considered putting you in that position."

Peter's body relaxed. He took a quick drink of coffee and set his cup down. "That's a relief, because it confirms an answer to our prayers. We would cherish any child in our home, and we actually gave some serious thought to making Ernest a member of our family." Peter reached for his wife's hand, and Sarah accepted his gesture. "But we're convinced that living with us is not in God's plan for him."

"That's because he's supposed to be with us," Lizzie said softly. Her eyes pleaded with Jack to explain.

"You all heard my spontaneous proposal the other night. Well, we've talked it over and decided. Lizzie and I want to marry and raise Ernest as our son." Jack's voice held a calmness she yearned to embrace.

"We'll talk to Reverend Brown tomorrow and inform him of our intentions and desire to adopt Ernest," Lizzie said, jumping in, eager to relay their plan before anyone had a chance to challenge their decisions. "We're not strangers to the orphanage, and we'll be able to provide a good home for Ernest, so I can't imagine the reverend would refuse."

"Peter, we'd like you to perform the ceremony, if you're willing." Jack was following Lizzie in not providing an opening for opinions until they'd finished explaining. "We thought if we had a simple wedding on Friday evening, it would give Lizzie's parents and her younger brother enough time to have responsibilities at their restaurant covered, and they could get here from Portland."

"Where are you holding the wedding?" Helen asked.

"Hopefully, we'll be able to use the chapel at Brown Hall," Lizzie said. "And I know it's a lot to ask, but could we gather here for a small celebration after? I'll take care of everything."

"My dear, you can hold a party and invite as many people as you want. But I insist on helping with the preparations. Emma and Julia will want to pitch in too. And if the chapel isn't feasible, you can also have the ceremony here."

"Thank you, Helen." Gratitude rushed through Lizzie. What would she do without her charitable friend?

"You know how much I care for you both, so I would be remiss if I didn't ask." Helen cocked her head. "Are you truly ready for this? You've only known each other for a short time. I don't want to see either of you regret this later."

"We have no qualms," Jack said with respect but also a firmness that assured Lizzie even more that she'd made the right decision.

Peter studied Jack, then his gaze caught Lizzie's for a moment. He leaned forward, pushed his empty plate out of the way, and laid folded hands on the table. What did the reverend have on his mind? "I know you want the best for Ernest, and I admire your loyalty to his mother."

Lizzie shot a glance at Jack. Where was Peter going with this?

"But it's important that you take any vows seriously. No marriage is like another, but you won't do the child any service if you aren't genuine in your own relationship." Peter unclasped his hands, then folded them together again. "Before I agree to marry you, I need to think and pray about my decision. I realize that time is limited—and so does the Lord. I'll give you my answer tomorrow morning."

Seventeen

D ressed in a new suit, Jack waited outside of Helen's home with his father, Peter, and Timothy, catching a breath in the cool October evening. Peter and Sarah had prayed all night after Jack and Lizzie requested him to officiate at their wedding.

By morning, Peter had felt at peace, and he agreed to marry them. His blessing gave Jack and Lizzie a sense of confirmation, and they were following through with their plan. But instead of holding the ceremony in the chapel at Brown Hall, they'd decided to keep things simple and say their vows here.

"I love you, Son." His father grabbed Jack's hand with a firmness that relayed the older man's strength and respect, but the moisture building in his eyes revealed the strong feelings behind the words. "And I'm happy for you."

"Thank you." Jack didn't have an example of a good marriage in his own home to draw upon, but he'd strive to be the caring parent his father had been.

"I should head in now and say hello to some folks." Dad patted him on the shoulder, then embraced him in a move that ended so abruptly, he questioned its reality as his father left his side.

Jack reached inside his jacket and patted the inner pocket. Still there—the emerald ring his grandmother had worn.

He'd asked why the ring hadn't been passed on to his brother, Adam, when he and Rose married. Dad had explained that before she died, she'd requested that Jack be given that piece of jewelry should he ever wed, since he was the oldest grandchild. Adam didn't mind, and he'd chosen an engagement ring in a style that suited Rose.

More sentimental than what he'd admit to most people, Jack was touched by his grandmother's gift. With so many other things on their minds, he and Lizzie hadn't talked about a ring. Hopefully, she'd be pleased and not bothered by his decision to surprise her during the ceremony.

Peter laid his hand on Jack's shoulder. "Would you mind if Timothy and I prayed for you?"

"I'd like that." Jack had never been asked that question before. He'd never thought he needed someone praying for him, but his life was changing, and he didn't know what to expect from here on.

The two men asked the Lord for patience, wisdom, and direction. As they continued, Jack's tense muscles relaxed, and a calmness fell over him. He wasn't in this journey alone. God would stand with him and provide guidance.

Peter closed the prayer, then gave Jack quick pats on his shoulder. "We don't always understand why God allows challenging situations, but we do know that he can bring good out of pain and disappointment. You and Lizzie love Ernest, and our heavenly Father does too. He has a design for that child's life, and Sarah and I are convinced that you're both to be a part of that plan."

"We're certainly willing to take the steps necessary to ensure that Ernest is safe and happy." Even to the extent of turning their lives upside down for him.

"And that's admirable." Peter peered into his eyes, as though he wanted to make sure Jack was paying attention. "But I've seen more between you and Lizzie than what you've been willing to admit. Don't shut your heart to love."

Jack nodded. He couldn't do or say more at that moment.

"We should go in." Timothy gave him a sly smile. In a few minutes, this man would become his brother-in-law, and hopefully, also a good friend. "You can't hide from my parents any longer, and I suggest you make the effort to see them ahead of your fiancée walking down the aisle."

Peter's eyebrows raised. "You haven't met them yet?"

Jack shrugged. "I'm not a coward, but you have to admit, our situation is a bit unusual. What father wants to be introduced to the man his daughter is marrying only minutes before the wedding?"

"Better now than later." Timothy chuckled, then grabbed Jack by the back of the neck and encouraged him toward the door.

Jack led the two men into the house where a small group had gathered in the parlor. A pretty woman held and fussed over Ernest as though the little boy was the most precious child she'd ever laid eyes on. Given her ginger-red hair and face sprinkled with freckles, no one could doubt she was Lizzie's mother.

"Come on. I'll introduce you." Timothy steered the way to the other side of the room. "Mother, I'd like you to meet Jack Butler, the man who will soon become your son-in-law. Jack, this is my mother, Johanna Clark."

"It's a pleasure, Mrs. Clark," Jack said. The mother-daughter resemblance was remarkable, except for Lizzie's lack of freckles. And in contrast to her striking green eyes, Mrs.

Clark's were a brilliant blue. "I realize our wedding might be a shock, and you probably have numerous questions for me. I promise I'll do my best to answer them all."

Mrs. Clark smiled. "I look forward to that. You have much to learn about us as well. After all, you are going to be a part of our family. You don't get Lizzie without the rest of us." She kissed the top of the baby's head. "Don't worry, Jack. I know my daughter. She wouldn't make such a hasty decision without believing it was the right thing for her, this child—*and* you."

A man with light brown hair graying at the temples joined them. Jack guessed him to be in his late forties. The older gentleman with piercing hazel eyes studied Jack as he extended his hand. "I'm Dennis Clark, Lizzie's father."

"I'm glad to meet you, sir." Jack returned the man's firm grip.

Mr. Clark cocked his head. "I met your father. He seems to be an intelligent, wise man. I hope you take after him."

"Dennis . . ." his wife said, in a tone that almost sounded reprimanding.

Jack glanced to the left where his dad was engaged in conversation with Helen.

Ernest whimpered, relaying some discomfort. "This baby either needs to be fed or changed, and I should check on Lizzie, so I'll leave you men alone." Mrs. Clark raised her eyebrows and gave her husband a glare that conveyed her expectation. He better demonstrate good behavior. Then she left the parlor with Ernest cradled in her arms.

"I don't have much to say, Jack, except that I love my daughter. If you don't treat her well, you'll have me to contend with," Mr. Clark said. "But as long as you do right by her, you'll be family and welcome in our home."

"Thank you, sir." He shook Mr. Clark's hand again. "I intend to do my best."

"Don't just try. Commit to it."

"Yes, sir," Jack swallowed. When was the last time he felt like a child? He would prove to them all that he was a man of his word, and he didn't take any vows lightly. But what was he getting himself into? Had Jack acted too quickly in proposing that he and Lizzie marry? Were they both being irrational?

Mr. Clark left and headed in Peter's direction, but Timothy remained.

"Your father is . . ." Jack needed to be careful in giving any definitions.

"Difficult. Hard. Intimidating. Protective." Timothy quirked a smile. "You don't need to tell me. But he can also be patient and generous." He rubbed his eyebrow with his thumb. "At least you've been spared Joseph's mischief—for today. He stayed behind to manage the restaurant in our parents' absence, but you won't be shielded forever."

"Thanks for the warning."

"I think there's something else you should know before this wedding takes place."

Jack released a heavy sigh. Another lecture?

"Don't worry, friend. I'm not about to threaten you. Trust me, Lizzie can hold her own."

"Then what?" As Jack's best man, did Timothy believe it was his duty to impart some encouragement—even wisdom?

"I've wondered if I should bring it up." He hesitated. "She told you about Alex."

"I know Lizzie loved him deeply—and still does."

"Alex will always have a part of Lizzie's heart. But that

doesn't mean there isn't room for someone else." Timothy's carefree tone had grown serious. "My sister has a great capacity to love—if you're patient and give her a chance."

"Lizzie is a loving person—toward many people."

"She cares more for you than you realize," Timothy said, keeping his voice low. "She may even be fooling herself. Lizzie would never have agreed to marry you, despite her concern for Ernest, if she didn't have feelings for you. My sister is creative and persistent. If she'd had any reservation about becoming your wife—she would have found another way for that child to have a family."

"Are you sure?"

"As sure as I am of anything, and if you think about it, you heard the same conviction from my mother."

Jack's heart beat heavy against his chest, but his spirit soared light and free.

Could that be true? Could Lizzie genuinely care for him?

Could this strange, unpredictable path for Lizzie, Ernest, and him be part of God's plan?

Eighteen

"Lizzie, you look—beautiful!"

"Thank you, Mother." Lizzie turned to view the back of her dress in the full-length mirror in Helen's bedroom. "I never dreamed—this is too much."

"Nonsense. You're our only daughter. I've imagined your wedding since you were born, and I wouldn't be denied this vision."

Her parents had arrived with wedding attire in hand. Lizzie had planned to wear a dress already hanging in her closet, but disappointing her mother wasn't an option. Besides, the elegant white gown with a band lace collar and a full skirt and veil trimmed in matching finery was too lovely to turn down.

As soon as the upcoming nuptials had been announced, her mother had visited their dressmaker in Portland. Mrs. Draper had Lizzie's measurements, and she'd altered and re-fashioned a garment hanging on display in her shop.

"Ernest was ready for a nap, so Emma took him back to the nursery at Brown Hall. She just returned." Her mother folded her hands in front of her and smiled.

"I wish he could be a part of this, but realistically, he isn't aware of what's happening. It would only be selfish of me to insist Emma keep him here." Lizzie stood full view in front of the mirror. "We'll sign adoption papers for Ernest on

Monday. In the meantime, he'll need to stay at the orphanage, so maybe it's best he's settled in for the night."

"Everyone is ready to start when you are," Julia said as she swept into the room carrying two bouquets, one much larger than the other. Heather was mixed in with various shades of chrysanthemums, all picked from Helen's gardens.

"Oh, the flowers are beautiful!" Tears burned Lizzie's eyes as a wave of unexpected sentiment swept through her. She wasn't taking imaginary steps. She was getting married, and the commitment was real—lasting.

Besides offering to make the floral arrangements, Helen had also baked and decorated a two-tiered wedding cake. The special gift was meant to be a surprise, but Lizzie had spotted it while making a quick trip to the kitchen for a glass of water. She'd hugged and thanked Helen for her generosity, and the older woman had blushed, insisting that creating the dessert had been a joy and an act of love.

Lizzie dried the moisture at the corner of her eyes with a white handkerchief, then she took a deep breath and smiled at her mother. "I'm ready."

Julia handed her the larger bouquet and kept the smaller one as her bridesmaid. Lizzie was grateful for Timothy agreeing to stand as best man. Hopefully, her brother's support helped to relieve her parents' reservations about her decision to marry Jack before they'd had a chance to even meet him.

The time had arrived. A friend of Helen's played a sweet melody on the violin as Lizzie accepted her father's arm and stepped into the parlor. Jack, Timothy, and Julia already stood in front of the fireplace where a garland made from mums and heather was draped. How thoughtful of Helen.

Lizzie's focus moved to Jack, and her breath caught. It

wasn't that she'd dismissed his good looks or tender heart before, but now—the way he stood straight in his suit, his smile as he welcomed her to his side, and the depth of emotion in his eyes—Lizzie was completely captured by the attraction stirring within her.

Peter proceeded with the ceremony, and Lizzie concentrated on each individual moment. They said their vows, and Peter turned to Jack. "The ring?"

Oh, no! They'd been so concerned about her family's arrival and adopting Ernest, they'd forgotten about this part of the ceremony. It wasn't imperative to finalizing their commitment to each other, and this wasn't a conventional marriage, so Lizzie didn't expect to be given a symbol of love. But Peter was unaware of a ring's absence, and now this oversight would be another indication to her father that Lizzie and Jack had made a hasty decision.

Jack opened his palm, revealing an emerald set in a feminine silver setting.

Lizzie stared into Jack's eyes, hoping to convey how much she appreciated his thoughtfulness. She held out her trembling hand, and he gently slipped it on her finger.

A few more words were said, and Peter pronounced them man and wife. Lizzie took a deep breath and prepared to face her family as a married woman, but Jack cupped her face with his hands. Was he going to kiss her—here and now—in front of everyone? Lizzie's heart pounded. Did she want him to?

He kissed her forehead gently, then taking her hand and intertwining her fingers with his, he led her into the center of the room, where their guests hugged and congratulated them.

Jack's affectionate kiss had shown his respect for her, and Lizzie appreciated the graceful way he handled that part of the wedding. She would have been taken aback if he'd kissed her on the mouth without warning.

Yet . . . what would have happened if he *had* kissed her lips? And why hadn't he? Had she been wrong about what she'd witnessed in his eyes? Maybe she'd only seen what she'd wanted to because of her own feelings.

Stop it, Lizzie! You either want him to care or you don't. You can't have it both ways

.

❧

Jack's house—*their* house—on the farm was small but cozy. Lizzie scanned the kitchen. The table with two chairs would suit them for now. Timothy had promised to craft a high chair for Ernest, but there was time for that. The little boy was only six weeks old.

Only six weeks! Their lives have been completely changed in that time!

A comfortable-looking rocking chair sat by the fireplace, and Jack had built a small fire after carrying the last of her belongings into the bedroom. The rest of her things had been delivered earlier that day. The home would serve them well until an addition could be built with two more bedrooms—one for Jack and one for Ernest. She'd plant flower beds in the spring. Lizzie had missed having her own gardens since moving to Brown Hall.

"Are you thirsty? Hungry?" Jack opened the ice box and peered inside.

"No, thank you. I'm fine."

"I stocked up on a few things, but we can make a list of what you'd like to have on hand tomorrow."

Lizzie ran her hand over the top of the rocking chair. "Timothy said he'd help with a crib. And we'll need to get diapers and other things for the baby, so we're prepared to bring him home." *Home.*

"Yes—of course." By Jack's expression, he'd registered the meaning as well. The responsibility of creating such a place for Ernest—for *them*—felt a bit daunting at the moment.

Lizzie fingered the emerald on her left hand.

"I hope I didn't take you off guard," Jack said, nodding toward the ring.

"No—well, a bit." Lizzie smiled. "We didn't talk about that tradition before the wedding, so the gift was a complete surprise." She held up her hand and admired the piece of jewelry. "It's so beautiful. Thank you. I truly love it."

The muscles in his face relaxed into a pleased grin. "Good. I'm glad. It was my grandmother's. She wanted my wife to have it."

His *wife*. Lizzie slipped into the rocking chair. "I will always cherish it."

He pulled up a chair from the table and sat across from her. "We'll get more furniture. A couple of soft chairs by the fire would be nice with winter ahead." He caught her gaze. "This place is yours, Lizzie. I want you to feel comfortable making changes as you see fit."

"Thanks, Jack."

They spent an hour talking about the wedding, plans for the next few days, and the impending adoption. Then he stood. "I better get up to the other house. We have a big day tomorrow, and we should both get some rest."

She walked him to the entrance. Jack stood there with the door open, hesitating. His eyes held the same longing Lizzie felt, and her breathing shallowed. For one brief moment, it felt like he might kiss her, and she moistened her lips in anticipation.

Instead, he stepped outside and broke the intense connection between them. She gasped in disappointment. "Good night, Lizzie." He walked away without a touch—without another word—without even looking back.

What did she expect? This wasn't a love match. They'd agreed to a contract in order to raise a child together.

But the way he'd looked at her—the ring—inviting her to make this house her home. A hot tear slid down Lizzie's face. It all felt so confusing. Why did he have to be so kind and generous? It would be easier to not care for him if he were stoic and stern.

How was Lizzie ever going to be the wife he needed and the mother Ernest deserved without making the mistake of giving her heart to someone who couldn't share his own?

Nineteen

Jack held Ernest in the rocking chair by the fireplace, the logs now ablaze and sending heat into the room that chilly October evening. The infant stirred, breaking free from his blanket as he stretched out his arms. His mouth opened wide, and he released a quiet yawn. How could someone this small have changed Jack's life so drastically in one day? In the few seconds it took to place his signature on a piece of paper, he'd become a father.

"The dishes are dried and put away." Lizzie bent over Jack's shoulder and peered at the child—their *son*—as he yawned once more. "Oh, sweet boy, the busy day has worn you out. I think it's best we put you to bed."

As Lizzie leaned in close to take Ernest, her light flowery fragrance filled Jack's senses, and he would have been content to remain in her presence, but she slipped away far too soon for his preference. "You must be tired as well after such a busy day with finalizing the adoption, bringing Ernest home, and then cooking supper for both of us." Jack smiled up at her. "Thank you. Thank you for all of it."

"You're welcome. And I'm not sleepy at all. This has been one of the best days of my life." She cuddled Ernest close to her chest. "It was nice of Timothy and Julia to want to join us in a celebration, but after the excitement of having our family and friends at the wedding, it seemed fitting for us three to spend time together as a family."

Yes, a family . . . Lizzie was a natural caretaker. Unlike his own mother, she would do everything she could to nurture her child. Jack might not be the kind of husband she deserved, but he'd try to make her happy. And he'd do his best to become the father their son needed.

"Since you're putting Ernest to bed, I'll head up to the big house for the night," Jack said.

"You don't need to go. He's almost asleep. It will just take a minute to tuck him in, and then we can sit and talk, if you'd like."

He wavered at the door. Lizzie sounded like she genuinely desired him to stay, and he wanted to—he did. But restraint seemed essential for their well-being. Lizzie still loved another man. She was here because of Ernest—not because of Jack and any feelings for him.

"I'm feeling a bit exhausted myself, and I have to get up early . . ."

"Oh, of course." She seemed disappointed. "You probably have things to catch up on since you were absent from the farm today."

He nodded. "I do, but I'll check in on you and Ernest in the morning." Jack opened the door, then turned back and smiled at her. "We're going to make this work. I promise."

She returned his smile. "I know."

"Good night." He stepped outside and closed the door behind him. Then he turned back and raised his hand to knock.

No . . . Lizzie needed time to herself. He dropped his arm to his side. She earned that much and more after selflessly giving up her chance to have a real marriage.

Jack hiked up the path to the big house, and being so

consumed in his thoughts, he almost ran over the dark form perched on the porch steps.

"Better look where you're going, Son."

"What are you doing out here?"

"Thinking." His father's voice had taken on a serious tone. Something was wrong. "You back from supper with Lizzie already?"

"Yeah."

"Hmmm . . ." His father let out a heavy sigh. "Thought you'd stay longer. If you're going to raise a son together . . ."

"You know it's not a real marriage—not in that way. Lizzie and I are friends with a shared purpose, that's all."

"Not so sure about that."

Jack sat next to his father and leaned against the porch step. "Why are you so interested in my relationship with her and what we do or don't do? Nothing is going to affect how I work on this farm."

"Oh, don't be foolish. I don't have any worries about your loyalty to me or this place. But I do see the way you and Lizzie look at each other. There's a longing between you two, and there's nothing wrong with that. As long as you don't waste the chance to be happy."

"I'm fine. And so is Lizzie." Jack heard paper rustling, but he couldn't make out the source in the dark. "What do you have there?"

"A letter."

"From?"

"I've been trying to figure out how to tell you something— something important."

Jack's instincts were right. Whatever was going on, he wasn't going to like it.

"Son, I've wanted to tell you and your brother for a long time, but I couldn't break my promise to your mother. But now . . . with this news . . . you have a right to know."

"Know what?" Why was Dad being so evasive? Jack wanted to reach inside his father and literally pull out the information the older man held back.

"Your mother didn't just run off and leave us because she stopped caring. She had problems. The kind that made her a danger to you and your brother."

"I don't understand." Jack gripped the edge of the step, anticipating difficult news.

"There were times when she saw things—heard things—that weren't there. Your mother couldn't tell the difference between what was real and what wasn't. Her moods changed without warning. In that state, she'd become hostile—aggressive."

"I don't remember any of that." Why didn't he? Jack tried to recall a memory that would correlate with his father's disclosure, but nothing . . .

"Maybe because she was lucid some days. But those phases became fewer, and your mother feared she might hurt you or Adam. Some people wanted me to send her away to an institution and forget about her, but I just couldn't do it. I loved her so much, Jack, I couldn't bear the thought of what doctors might do to her.

"Your mother knew she was sick and that she was getting worse, so during a time when she had more clarity, she insisted on being committed to a hospital before her behavior became life-threatening. She never wanted you boys to know, and she made me promise not to tell you. She didn't want you visiting and seeing her that way—becoming more of a crazy woman."

"She'd rather we believe that she just left us?" Jack could have endured the truth far more than the lie he'd accepted all these years. All that time wasted, imagining his mother hadn't loved them enough to stay. That she'd viewed their family as only a burden, and being selfish, wanted a life for herself without any responsibility.

"I understand why her decision doesn't make sense, and I carry some regret at not telling you and Adam before now." His father rubbed his jaw. "Neither of us were thinking clearly back then. More recently, this particular illness has been given a name—schizophrenia. People with the condition usually aren't aware that they have it until a doctor or therapist tells them. They won't even realize that something is seriously wrong, so the fact that your mother recognized it is uncommon."

Questions exploded in Jack's brain. "So where has she been all this time? Have you visited?"

"Western State Hospital. Close enough that I could slip away occasionally and see how she was doing."

"I'm going there—to see her." Now that Jack knew the facts, how could he not? No longer was he going to guess where his mother had been, what she'd been doing all these years. He'd find out for himself.

"That's not possible." His father's voice revealed the pain behind his words. "This notice . . . your mother passed away yesterday, and if I want a choice in where she's buried, I need to claim her body tomorrow."

"Then I'm going with you. I won't let you go through this alone."

His father hunched over, and his body shook from

escaping sobs. "Your mother loved you boys, and she wanted you to know that."

Jack's mouth went dry. What could he say to relieve Dad's heartbreak? Jack had never witnessed his father shed even a tear, and now he displayed rare, raw emotion.

Dad sat up, sniffed, and swiped his arm beneath his nose. "I hope you can forgive me for not telling you the real story before now. If you can't, I understand. But please forgive your mother. She could have stayed. Made our lives miserable—even more painful than what her absence did. But she sacrificed herself to make it easier on you. Trust me, Jack. Your mother did the best she could. She spared you—spared all of us."

"So many years lost." Would it have made a difference if he'd known? Jack grasped the doors to his heart that had only recently cracked open. Maybe he should close them again and just go numb. It might be better to not feel anything than to feel the betrayal he suffered right now.

"I'm begging you. Don't waste any more time shutting yourself off or you'll end up a lonely man. Lizzie loves you. I know it. And you love her. She's not responsible for the choices your parents made and neither are you."

"Dad . . ."

"It's up to you, Son. You're in charge of the path you take from here. What kind of life do you want for yourself? What kind of life do you think *God* wants for you?"

Twenty

Lizzie felt a warm hand on her shoulder as she moved a wooden spoon around a large kettle of chicken soup on the stove. She blinked, emerging from her mental fog.

"Are you all right?" Helen asked. "I don't think you've heard a word I've said. You've been stirring that pot for the last few minutes as though hypnotized by the motion."

"I'm sorry." Lizzie laid the spoon on the counter and smoothed her apron. A second batch of soup simmered next to the first. She'd check it in a moment. "My mind wandered elsewhere. Does Ernest need tending?"

"No, he's fine. Still asleep. No one has claimed your old bedroom yet, and being next to the kitchen, it's the perfect place for him to nap." Helen leaned toward the stove and inhaled the food's aroma. "I was talking about how excited the children are after being told they'll have one more day at the expo."

Lizzie opened the cupboard and reached for a stack of bowls. "That's right . . . it closes soon."

"October sixteenth—twelve more days." Helen placed a loaf of freshly baked bread on a cutting board with five more to follow. "Are you and Jack planning on spending more time at the fair?"

"I don't know. Attending the expo may not be a priority for him right now." Other serious and important topics had consumed their conversations since the truth about his mother had been revealed three nights earlier.

Helen stopped slicing bread. "I don't mean to overstep, but you haven't been yourself the past couple of days. Are you and Jack having problems? You both seemed so happy on Monday when you signed the adoption papers."

"Oh, there's no need to worry about us." At least not *yet*. Lizzie sighed. Now was as good a time as any. She needed to talk to someone, and Jack and his father had given her permission that morning to share the news about Mary Butler with Helen. "We've spent our evenings together with Ernest, and after we get him to bed, Jack has stayed for hours. It's been nice to feel close to him."

Their intimate discussions had been wonderful, and the unexpected ways he'd touched her had endeared him to Lizzie. Not in the way a husband would reach for a wife—but the gentle hand on her back or shoulder, however brief, made her feel cherished.

Helen's brow furrowed. "Then what's on your mind? Why the gloomy face?"

"My heart aches for Jack. He found out the night of the adoption that his father has been lying about his mother." Lizzie explained where Mary Butler had lived for years and why.

"Oh, my goodness." Helen sunk onto a chair near the table. "I can't imagine the burden LeRoy has been carrying all these years. And now Jack finding out the truth. He must have been so hurt and angry."

"He loves his father and has forgiven him, but it's going to take a while for emotional wounds and their relationship to heal." Lizzie managed a weak smile. "However, Jack has been willing to pray with me, and I've noticed a softening in him."

"Then God is working through this. Amen to that." Helen tapped the table three times with her finger. "And Adam? Does he know?"

"They sent word, and he was present to help bury her at the cemetery. It was a quiet service with our small family." *Family.* She belonged to theirs now. "No one else was informed. Mr. Butler wanted to honor his wife, but his sons were dealing with enough without being questioned by people."

"I'm sorry I'm late," Emma said, rushing into the kitchen. "I'm here to help with supper now, and Rachel is right behind me. But, Lizzie, there's a phone call for you."

"Thanks, Emma," Lizzie said, untying her apron. Was someone in trouble, hurt—or worse? One phone existed in the building, and it had been placed in the main office. No one had called her before, not even her mother. Lizzie sprinted down the hall and into the room.

She put the receiver next to her ear and spoke into the mouthpiece on the candlestick base. "Hello? This is Lizzie." She almost gave her last name as Clark, but that was no longer true.

"Lizzie, it's so good to hear you. This is Nellie—Nellie Wick." The familiar voice came through the line loud and clear.

The receiver almost slipped from Lizzie's fingers. Seven weeks had passed since Nellie left Ernest at the orphanage, and there hadn't been a word from her since. Why was she calling now? Did she expect to stroll in like nothing had happened? As though she hadn't abandoned her baby and asked Lizzie to take care of him?

"Are you there?" Nellie asked, sounding worried.

"Yes, I'm here." Lizzie closed her eyes and took a deep breath. "You must be calling about Ernest. He's wonderful, Nellie. He's a delightful little boy." She heard a relieved sigh.

"I'm so glad." Painful silence filled what felt like an hour, but in reality, lasted only seconds. "Thank you for watching over him."

"It's what you asked. It was the right thing to do, and I'm very fond of him. We all are." Fond? No, Lizzie *loved* that child as much as if she'd borne him herself.

"I miss him terribly, and I'd like to see him—on Sunday. My mother and father will come with me. They're anxious to meet their grandson."

The announcement blasted through the line like a locomotive out of control, and Lizzie's knees buckled. She swallowed and willed her next words to pass through her lips. "He won't be here."

"What do you mean?"

"I've adopted him—*we've* adopted him—to protect Ernest." Lizzie waited, holding her breath.

"You said *we*."

"Your childhood friend, Jack Butler, cares deeply for your son." *Our* son. "And we recently married so we could raise him together."

"Jack?"

Lizzie heard Nellie crying softly on the other end of the line, and her own tears pooled. "This all must be a shock. I'm so sorry. We thought we were doing the right thing—the best thing for Ernest."

"Where are you living?" Nellie sniffed, but she didn't sound hurt or angry.

"On Jack's farm. Ernest and I are staying in the small house, and Jack is with his father. But Jack will move in with us once he's able to build an addition." Why did Lizzie offer so much information? She didn't want to hurt anyone, but didn't Nellie deserve the truth?

"I know the farm. It's beautiful."

"Nellie, please bring your parents there on Sunday. Come at noon, and we'll have dinner together."

"Thank you, but I don't want to be an imposition. We'll come at two, if that would be all right."

"Yes, that's fine."

"Thank you. We—we have a lot to talk about."

Lizzie heard a soft sob and then a click.

൬

"Jack, what if Nellie wants Ernest back?" Lizzie didn't miss the flicker of pain in her new husband's eyes as she mentioned that strong possibility. Clearly, he felt the same threat as they discussed the latest revelation affecting their lives.

"So many questions yet to be answered. We don't know her reasons for giving him up, or why she decided to suddenly reappear after two months." Jack reached for her hand.

She accepted the tender gesture. How warm and reassuring his grasp felt. "That's true. Nellie gave no indication of why she's coming now, except to see her son and talk." Perhaps their new little family wouldn't be separated.

"We took on the responsibility of raising Ernest out of loyalty to her and wanting to ensure her son's future. That's always been our priority."

Lizzie's vision blurred as realization settled in her heart.

"So, if she wants Ernest, it's only right that we return him to his mother—for his sake and hers." A tear escaped the pool forming in her eyes, and it left a hot trail down her cheek. Lizzie wiped the moisture from her face.

Jack squeezed her hand and nodded. "Nellie won't be here for two more days. I think we should spend as much time as possible with Ernest before then."

"And also pray." Lizzie took a deep breath. Would Jack be willing to pray together? Proverbs 3:5–6 came to mind. "The Bible says, 'Trust in the Lord with all thine heart; and lean not unto thine own understanding. In all thy ways acknowledge him, and he shall direct thy paths.'"

"So we should trust God—have faith that he knows what's best for all of us. And if we ask, he'll show us what to do."

Lizzie searched his eyes. "Do you believe that?"

"Trust doesn't come easy for me."

"I know you've been let down in the past. So have I, but I've realized something these past months. Sometimes, no matter how hard people try, they either have no choice or they just don't know how to make good on their promises. That's why we need to put our trust in God and not in anything or anyone else. He's not going to fail us."

Jack nodded. "I'll pray. And I'll do my best to accept the outcome." He covered their entwined hands with his other. "I don't think we have any time to waste."

"Thank you," she whispered as he bowed his head.

As he talked to the Lord with the ease of an old friend, but still with reverence, Lizzie was taken aback by how little she knew about Jack's faith. Had he been testing her to see if her own was on solid ground?

Grateful that they were in harmony in their approach to

Nellie's visit, Lizzie still pondered what it would mean for her and Jack's relationship. They'd wed to provide Ernest a caring family, but they hadn't consummated their marriage. If Nellie took her son, would it only be fair to release Jack and allow him to find someone he could truly love?

Twenty-One

J ack, needing a moment to collect the whirl of random thoughts and emotions unexpectedly assailing him, hung back after greetings were exchanged that following Sunday. Lizzie assisted Nellie and her aging mother to the settee. Mr. Wick, using a cane, shuffled to the comfortable, soft chair offered.

As a child, Nellie had always been slim, but now her dress hung on her thin body. Raven hair still framed her face, and the scar that ran along her left eye was a reminder of the fall she'd taken while on one of their adventures. Her pale skin and the dark circles beneath her deep brown eyes hinted that she was not well.

"May I see him?" Nellie asked, sounding anxious, not waiting for Lizzie to even offer coffee or tea.

Lizzie glanced at Jack. "Of course. Ernest woke from a nap a short time ago and has been fed. I'd laid him in his crib while I tended to his wet diaper, and then we heard you arrive." Her lips quivered.

Aware that she might be saying goodbye to the little boy, Lizzie must be struggling to keep herself together. If they were asked to give up the child, Jack would do whatever he could to ease her pain. "I'll get Ernest," he offered.

He went into the small bedroom and stood next to the crib. The infant lifted his arms above him and swung at the air.

Then Ernest turned his face toward Jack and kicked harder. In recognition of the man towering over him? Did he know how much his adoptive father had grown to love him?

Jack picked up the little boy and hugged him close to his chest. Then he said a silent prayer for strength and wisdom before carrying the baby into the other room.

Nellie's face lit up, and she reached out before Jack neared the settee. Her eyes glistened with moisture as he laid Ernest in her embrace. She cradled him, looking like the mother she was—or perhaps desired to be.

"Oh, my dear boy," she whispered. Nellie's countenance brightened. "Look! He's smiling!"

Jack bent over to catch whatever she was observing, and Lizzie rushed to do the same.

"He *is* smiling! He hasn't done this before." Lizzie beamed like the proud mother that she was—and wished to be. "Ernest waited until you could share in this special moment."

"Please tell me everything," Nellie begged in a tone that relayed her eagerness to learn all she could—details she'd missed while separated from her baby.

Lizzie retrieved a small rattle and held it near Ernest's right hand. He grabbed the toy and shook it, creating noise that excited him. "He's a strong little boy," she said, and she exchanged a smile with Nellie. Then Lizzie grew sober. "I suppose you're here to take him home with you."

"No," Nellie said sadly. "I only came to make sure Ernest was all right, to thank you, and to say goodbye."

♲

Had Lizzie heard correctly? Nellie didn't intend to reclaim her son? Relief mixed with grief for the little boy. Would Ernest one day feel a void—a loss—at not being raised by his real mother?

"I think they deserve an explanation, my dear," Mrs. Wick said, leaning close to her daughter and gently caressing the baby's head.

"Lizzie, I'm so sorry to have laid responsibility for Ernest on your shoulders." Nellie gave a small sigh. "I was desperate and had nowhere else to turn."

"I'm your friend. You could have asked for my help without leaving Ernest behind." There was no doubt that she loved her child. Lizzie would have done anything to keep them together if Nellie had come to her from the start.

"I know that now, but I wasn't in my right mind after giving birth." Nellie closed her eyes for a moment as though gathering strength to continue her story. "I did my best to hide my condition, but I was already quite ill before I delivered Ernest. I knew I couldn't take care of him myself, but I also refused to give up hope that somehow my situation would get better—*I'd* get better. A small part of me believed I would return for him."

Nellie chewed her lower lip, and she looked at Lizzie apologetically. "You probably thought the letter I left behind with him was vague, and it was meant to be. I wanted you to keep him under your guardianship until my circumstances changed. That wasn't fair, but like I said, I wasn't thinking clearly."

She turned to her father, and he gave an encouraging nod for her to continue.

"After leaving Ernest, I returned to my parents' home to make amends with them. They have cared for me and seen to my medical needs."

"And the doctors are helping you?" Jack asked, his deep concern ringing through his tone.

Nellie shook her head. "I'm dying, Jack. Nothing more can be done."

His shoulders slumped.

If Lizzie had been standing, her knees would have given out, and she would have dropped to the floor. "Nellie . . ." She had no words to describe her sorrow.

"I'm so sorry." Jack, still standing, grabbed the back of a nearby chair. "The boy's father?"

Nellie shook her head. "Broken promises." Pain flickered in her eyes. "You won't ever have to worry about him."

So the man cared nothing about Nellie or their son. That revelation sparked heated anger in Lizzie's belly, but a wave of relief doused the rage. Ernest wouldn't be subjected to living with a man who couldn't offer him what he needed and deserved. "And Ernest?"

"My parents have agreed that at their age and being in poor health themselves, they're not in a position to take care of a small child and raise him to manhood." Nellie gave her mother a tender smile. "But they are willing to walk me through my last days." Her gaze moved between Jack and Lizzie. "I came to say goodbye to Ernest—and you both. I won't be returning." Nellie's voice hitched with that last declaration.

"Goodbye?" The air rushed from Lizzie's lungs. How could Nellie not want to spend every last moment with her precious son?

"I don't want to put more on your shoulders than what I've already asked of you," Nellie said, her breathing now sounding labored. "But you cannot imagine the peace and joy I received when I learned that my dearest new friend and my closest childhood friend had found each other and not only fallen in love and married, but that they'd also adopted my little boy."

Nellie raised Ernest higher so she could bend down and kiss his cheek. "I wept and praised God for his goodness in providing more than what I could ever have imagined for my baby." Silent tears streamed down her face as she gazed upon him.

"Of—of course, we'll raise Ernest. We *love* him." Lizzie's heart broke at watching Nellie willingly and unselfishly give up her child once again—this time for good.

"I—we—have a request." Nellie looked to Jack this time.

"Anything," he said with a husky voice.

"My parents would appreciate permission to visit occasionally. They'd like to spend time with Ernest and be a part of his life."

Jack caught Lizzie's eye and she nodded, giving her consent. "Mr. and Mrs. Wick, you'll always be welcome here." He stepped toward Mr. Wick and extended his hand for a shake, sealing the deal.

Nellie and her parents, savoring every moment with Ernest, stayed into the evening. Lizzie had insisted they remain for a light supper, and those few hours together also gave Jack and Nellie an opportunity to restore their friendship, share stories, and heal old wounds.

But after Lizzie climbed into bed alone that night, unable to sleep, she moved to bended knee moments later in prayer. Questions no longer remained as to whether Nellie would return or not. No turning back now. Lizzie and Jack would raise

Ernest together.

Everything pointed to God leading them to that place. But how was she going to survive marriage to a man she loved— yes, *loved*—who didn't feel the same way about her?

<h1 style="text-align:center">Twenty-Two</h1>

C heerful light flooded the front room as the sun continued to rise—her favorite time of day. Lizzie especially
appreciated the bright rays after two gray, rainy days. With
Ernest taking his morning nap, she was free to nestle into the
settee for her daily Bible reading and prayer.

She'd grown lax with this ritual long before, but since
Nellie's visit six days ago, Lizzie had found solace in reading
Scripture and conversing with her heavenly Father. Devoted
to Jack and Ernest, she felt the weight of her undertaking and
asked for strength. She would continue loving them both,
whether or not her feelings were ever reciprocated.

A knock came at the door, and Lizzie set her Bible aside.
After two weeks of marriage, Jack still insisted on asking permission to enter his own home. It was sweet of him to be so
considerate of her privacy, but they would soon dwell in the
same house, and he should feel comfortable coming and going
as he pleased.

"Good morning!" Lizzie said as she opened the door and
stepped aside so her husband could enter. "There's hot coffee
on the stove. Would you like some?"

"No, thank you." Jack removed his hat and held it in front
of him as if he were nervous. Except, why should he be?

"It's such a beautiful Saturday. Are you working on the
bedroom today?" If so, the pounding might bother Ernest, but

she could take their son to Brown Hall for a quiet afternoon nap. Helen might also appreciate an extra pair of hands in the kitchen.

"No, but Dad and I plan to have it done by next Friday, and then I'll move in here with you and Ernest. If you're comfortable with that."

"This is your home, Jack. You have every right to live here."

"Of course, I'll keep my promise and stay in the new bedroom. Once Ernest needs his own room, we may exchange houses with my dad. He and I talked this morning, and that seems to make the most sense, as he doesn't need a place that big for himself."

The large farmhouse would give them ample space, and she'd already come up with ideas for making it more comfortable and homier, but Lizzie also felt unexpectedly attached to her current accommodations. And it wasn't like there would be any additions to their family—not with Jack determined to keep emotional and physical distance.

These past two weeks, the two of them had spent many hours together, and they'd grown closer after he relayed the truth about his mother, and even more so after Nellie's visit. But Lizzie sensed that although Jack enjoyed their deepening friendship, something still kept him from opening his heart to her fully.

She'd also protected herself and refrained from giving hers completely to him. Love for Alex wasn't holding her back. Not any longer. She'd always be grateful for what they shared, and she would remember him, but not with the same ache as before.

Here and now, Lizzie cared so much for Jack, she feared

rejection and losing the intimacy they'd created. She trusted his commitment to their new family, but what if Nellie had taken her son?

"Today is the final day of the expo, Lizzie. I'd like to take you and stay into the evening."

"What about Ernest?" Although an area at the exposition had been designated as a nursery for nurses and other staff to care for small children while their parents explored the fair, Lizzie couldn't imagine leaving their two-month-old there.

"It's arranged. Julia and Timothy will be here in an hour to stay with him."

"You made that decision without asking me?" Lizzie asked in a biting tone she immediately regretted. She trusted her brother and Julia. Why was she feeling a bit offended?

Jack stiffened. "I wanted to surprise you. These past weeks have been a bit challenging and stressful for both of us." He shoved his hand through his hair. "I thought it would be nice for us to have an outing together. The expo is closing, and we'll never get another chance to experience anything like it."

"I apologize. I shouldn't have reacted that way." Lizzie smiled and put her hand lightly on his arm. "Your gesture was unexpected, that's all. It was very considerate of you to plan an outing for us, as well as the baby's care."

His body visibly relaxed, and he gave her a mischievous grin. "We deserve some fun."

"I agree, and I would enjoy spending the day with you." More than he could know—more than what she would ever confess.

∾

They'd spent the afternoon on the Pay Streak, each of them choosing amusement rides and games. While enjoying the Ferris wheel, Lizzie had snuggled in close to Jack, and though he'd wanted to hold her hand, he'd resisted, hoping that once plans were revealed, he'd have the courage to expose his heart.

At one end of the grounds, canoe races were being held on Lake Union between Northwest coastal tribes. Jack and Lizzie cheered for them all, not having a favorite in the competition. Then he suggested a ride in a gondola and was pleased when she agreed with enthusiasm. College boys served as gondoliers, and Lizzie kept up a lively conversation with their own.

Jack watched her with admiration. Everywhere she went, heads turned. Not only because she possessed the beauty of a mythical goddess with copper curls piled on top of her head, but he imagined also because of the way she carried herself—with dignity, yet an unassuming air of warmth and kindness.

As the sun was setting, the fairgrounds lit up with a hundred and fifty thousand electrical lights that would be turned off for the last time at midnight, after the closing ceremonies.

"I wanted you to see this one last time." Jack waved his arm around at the electrical display surrounding them.

She grinned and sighed. "It's truly magical. Thank you—for everything."

"It's been a real pleasure." He tilted his head. "Are you willing to try something new?"

"What do you have in mind?" she asked, raising her eyebrows.

From what he'd witnessed about her, Jack had no doubt she wouldn't hesitate to try unfamiliar foods and entertainment. "Dinner at Chinese Village. Afterward, we could attend a show at the Chinese Theater. The performers are from Chang Hi. What do you think?"

Lizzie's eyes lit up before he'd even finished explaining. "I think yes!"

His shoulders released some tension. A meal and a performance would provide conversation and distraction before he would need to disclose his intentions and why he'd wanted time alone with her tonight.

❧

Midnight drew near. Lizzie had never lived a more perfect day. Jack had been considerate at every turn, and she'd been elated to discover they shared a similar sense of humor. Their verbal exchanges had previously focused on more serious matters, but today she felt free in sharing another side of herself. The result had been ongoing laughter between them.

They strolled by a Dixieland band playing a lively tune, and Jack took her hand and spun her around. Lizzie delighted at the unexpected move. "You continue to surprise me, Mr. Butler."

"And you're not only beautiful, you're also light on your feet, Mrs. Butler."

His compliments and engaging warm smile created a flush of heat in Lizzie, and she instinctively put her hand to her hot face to cool the blush.

"There's another band playing in the pavilion up ahead. Would it shock you if I knew how to waltz?"

Lizzie laughed. "Another revelation! There seems to be much I have yet to learn about you, but if you're asking me to dance, I accept the invitation."

They entered the building where numerous couples swayed to classical music played by the orchestra. Jack led Lizzie into the mix, then holding her right hand, he placed his free hand on the curve of her back. They moved together, gliding across the floor. The two had never been so physically close, and although a small, proper distance remained between them, Lizzie believed their hearts beat in rhythm.

The two spun around the room for three more dances, maneuvering between other couples and making light conversation. Then the orchestra's director announced that closing ceremonies would commence soon, along with a fireworks display at Lake Union.

"Should we head over there?" Jack slowly released his hold on Lizzie, and she reluctantly stepped back, already missing his touch.

She nodded with sincere enthusiasm. If remaining in his arms wasn't an option, viewing the promised spectacle would be a wonderful way to end the evening.

It took less time than Lizzie expected to reach the lake. Rather than stand in the middle of the gathering crowd, Jack led her to an area a small distance away from the majority of people who listened to a gentleman giving a speech on a small stage set up near the water's edge. Seconds later the heavens over the lake lit up with explosions of color, and the night air filled with clapping and cheers.

Her breath caught. "It's like rainbows shattering into thousands of dazzling sparkles."

Jack reached for her hand. She accepted his warm, strong clasp and smiled up at him. His eyes reflected the radiant bursts in the sky.

"Lizzie, I don't want to live this way anymore—the way we

have these past weeks. I don't want a marriage like this," he said in a serious tone, just loud enough for her to hear above the noisy crowd and rockets.

Her heart pounded, and her breath quickened. Did he want their marriage annulled? How could he ask that of her after all they'd gone through together? Had their day at the expo only been a way to soften his declaration?

"You want to break our vows and go our separate ways?" Lizzie struggled to push the words through her lips. "What about Ernest?"

"No, that's not what I'm asking. You misunderstood my intentions." Jack's voice sounded pained, and he clenched her hand tighter. "I don't want us to live together as friends. I want us to be husband and wife—in all ways." He gently brushed a fallen curl from her eyes. "I love you."

She swallowed a sob of relief. "You do?"

He released her hand only to use both of his to cradle her face. Jack peered down at her. "I do, and I want us to be a real family. I know we've only known each other for a short time, but we belong together."

"I believe that too." Lizzie's joy soared with the atmosphere's blazing display. "I love you, and I want to be a wife who honors you and is the kind of helpmate you deserve."

Jack bent down and briefly touched his lips to hers with tenderness. Love's first kiss. He drew her close to his chest and kissed the top of her head. "I wanted today to be special and a new start to our lives together."

"It's been perfect." Lizzie would have been happy to linger in his embrace, but despite being somewhat hidden by darkness, they remained in public view. So she didn't protest when he freed her from his hold.

"It will feel even better after I tell you my plans—at least, I hope it will." Jack's voice held a mix of excitement and apprehension. "I've purchased a bit more land next to our farm—something I've been trying to accomplish for years. It's perfect for growing crops. And my father has agreed to selling our produce at Pike Place Market. I can finally expand our business."

"That's wonderful. I'm so happy for you."

"That's not all. I haven't forgotten my promise to you. There's a small space open in a building down a block from the market. I was thinking it might be the perfect spot for a café. It needs a lot of work, we'd have to invest in everything you'd need to make it functional, and it wouldn't be like your parents' large restaurant, but if you like it, it could be a good start."

Tears stung Lizzie's eyes. "With all that you've been dealing with—the news about your mother and Nellie—you've still been considering my dreams."

"You can trust me to keep my promises." His thumb trailed the curve of her neck, sending waves of desire through her body.

"Your idea for a café sounds ideal. With all the people visiting the market, some are sure to want a place to eat and relax." Yet, there was someone else to take into account. "We also have Ernest to think about. I can't run a business and care for him without some help. Leaving him with Julia at the orphanage won't be an option if I'm no longer employed there."

"We can hire someone. I'm willing to do whatever is necessary to make this work."

"Emma is seventeen, and she'll have no choice but to leave Brown Hall soon because of her age. She'll need to find employment somewhere. What if we hired her to help with both Ernest and the café?" Lizzie sighed. "Of course, finding a place to live might be difficult for her at first."

"If you're willing to move into the big house now, there's plenty of room for her to stay with us until she finds a place of her own, no matter how long it takes."

"You'd really do that for her?" Lizzie asked, stunned. The man she loved was even more generous than what she believed an hour ago.

"Not just for her—for all of us." He took her hands in his. "I've believed for years that I couldn't share my heart with a woman out of fear of being hurt. But you've taught me that I can and that it's worth the risk." Jack brought her clasped fingers to his warm lips for a brief kiss, then held their joined hands to his chest. "These past months, I've witnessed how God has worked on my behalf, even when I wasn't aware. Wounds are healing, and I owe that to you and to him."

She leaned into her husband—her love. "I've discovered some things about myself too. I've depended on myself, afraid to ask anyone for help, even God. But you and friends at the orphanage have shown me that I don't have to be alone in anything."

"I promise to always come to you with a trusting heart, Lizzie Butler."

"As will I, Jack Butler." Lizzie smiled up at him.

He grinned in the glow of cascading illuminations. Then Jack kissed her with passion and sealed their promises.

Dear Reader,

I've lived in the Seattle area for twenty-eight years and have made many trips to the top of the Space Needle—a city landmark since the world's fair held here in 1962. But I was unaware of the fascinating events that took place at the 1909 Alaska-Yukon-Pacific Exposition until I watched a special presentation on PBS. My imagination immediately began to create possible scenarios, and I began to research what transpired during that time.

What I discovered blew my mind! The truth? The Children's Home Society of Washington State did indeed raffle off a month-old baby named Ernest. The infant was left at Brown Hall, an orphanage run by the organization. But he was never claimed by the ticket winner, and although no one has shown documented proof, it's likely that he was returned to the orphanage and later adopted. The building on the cover of *With a Trusting Heart* is an actual photo of Brown Hall in 1909.

In today's world, we would be appalled at hearing a baby could be used as a prize; however, there was a time when children were not as valued as they are today. Similar to what happened to Ernest, in an effort to raise money and find homes for orphaned children, a Paris foundling hospital held a raffle of live babies in 1911.

The children found homes, and proceeds were divided among several charitable institutions. The winners were investigated to make sure they would be desirable parents. That event happened two years after the expo took place, but I felt that by taking liberties with the date in my story, I could help readers accept the reality of Ernest also being raffled.

If you've read my historical romance series, The Daughters of Riverton, you may have been surprised—and hopefully, delighted—by the appearance of Peter and Sarah Caswell in this book. For those of you who were just introduced to them . . . are you curious about their lives and romance? I encourage you to read *Sarah's Smile*, the first novel in the series.

My hope is that you were transported through my words back to 1909 and the fair. My prayer is that you were encouraged through Lizzie's and Jack's experiences to trust that God is still in control. Even when we can't see a way for situations to work out, our heavenly Father will often reveal answers that are far better than what we could conceive on our own. I know that to be true in my own life.

God bless!
Dawn

Acknowledgements

Readers . . . You are appreciated more than you can imagine. Your interest in my stories gives me purpose, and the loving support you continue to offer warms my heart.

Annette M. Irby & Ocieanna Fleiss . . . Writers understand writers, and you have walked this journey with me for over a decade. I rely on you in so many ways!

Sandra Ardoin . . . Our relationship—both personal and professional—continues to bless me. I didn't set out to write a story that included characters from my Daughters of Riverton series, but after sharing this story's plot with you and the timing, you suggested a cameo appearance. I loved that idea! It was Peter and Sarah who decided that if they were going to make the long trip from Wisconsin to Seattle, they deserved more significant roles than what a few paragraphs could offer. Characters often direct authors!

Tina Boyd & Leann St. Germain . . . You always have my back.

Sonny . . . You know I would never have become an author without your support. Thanks for all the delicious dinners that were ready for me after a long day at the computer. I love you! And not just for your cooking skills!

God, my Father . . . Thank you for ALL things. You have provided me a full life and avenues to pursue my dreams.

Meet the Author

Dawn Kinzer, a mom and grandmother, lives with her husband in the beautiful Pacific Northwest. Favorite things include dark chocolate, cinnamon, popcorn, strong coffee, a good wine, the mountains, family time, and *Masterpiece Theatre*.

You can find out more about Dawn and her books by visiting www.dawnkinzer.com.

She loves to hear from her readers. You may contact her at dawn@dawnkinzer.com.

Other places to connect: Facebook, Goodreads, Pinterest, BookBub, Amazon Author Page, and Instagram

FREEBIE! Download "Maggie's Miracle"—a short story—as a gift when you visit www.dawnkinzer.com and sign up to receive Dawn's author newsletter sharing interesting tidbits about her books, photos, and other fun stuff about her writing world. Also available for purchase on Kindle.

The Daughters of Riverton

Historical Romance Series

Take a trip back to the early 1900s and spend time in the small farming community of Riverton, Wisconsin, where people find the courage to forgive, pursue their dreams—and love.

Book 1 – ***Sarah's Smile***

Book 2 – ***Hope's Design***

Book 3 – ***Rebecca's Song***

Though they follow a time sequence with some characters playing a role in every story, each book is a stand-alone romance featuring a different couple.

Questions that can be used for self-reflection or discussion are included at the end of each story.

Available in ebook and paperback on Amazon.
Available in paperback on Barnes & Noble.com
and Books-A- Million. com

By All Appearances

*An attractive special events planner
is determined to keep her distance.
A disfigured musician struggles to guard his heart.
By all appearances, both are destined to fail.*

Available in ebook and paperback on Amazon.
Available in paperback on Barnes & Noble.com
and Books-A- Million.com

A Night Divine

A popular model eager to find purpose.
An outreach minister with a hidden past.
A tragedy bound them together.
But will the truth tear them apart?

Available in ebook and paperback on Amazon.
Available in paperback on Barnes & Noble.com
and Books-A- Million.com